THE GUNSMITH

457

The Guns of St. Augustine

Books by J.R. Roberts
(Robert J. Randisi)

The Gunsmith series

Lady Gunsmith series

Angel Eyes series

Tracker series

Mountain Jack Pike series

COMING SOON!

The Gunsmith
458 – The Gunsmith Saloon

For more information visit:
www.SpeakingVolumes.us

THE GUNSMITH

457

The Guns of St. Augustine

J.R. Roberts

SPEAKING VOLUMES, LLC
NAPLES, FLORIDA
2020

The Guns of St. Augustine

ISBN 978-1-64540-208-4

Chapter One

"Once," Clint said.

"Once?"

"A long time ago."

"What took the Gunsmith to Florida?" General George Hammond asked.

"General," Clint said, "I actually can't remember. It was that long ago."

"Well," Hammond said, "it doesn't really matter. We're just very grateful that you agreed to come to Washington for this meeting."

"I came because Jim West asked me to."

"That's understood," Hammond said. "Mr. West is on a very important assignment of his own. But in point of fact, you were specifically requested for this mission by someone else."

"Oh?" Clint asked. "Who?"

"Geronimo."

***

The summons to Washington had come to him in a telegram while he was in Denver. He had gone there to visit his friend, Talbot Roper, only to discover that Roper was away, on a case. Clint considered Tal Roper to be the finest private detective in the country. He wasn't surprised to find that he was working.

He remained in Denver for several days, which was the reason the telegram, first sent to Labyrinth, Texas, caught up to him.

During his time there, he met a woman named Samantha Carlson. They were having supper in the same restaurant and their eyes met across the room. Within an hour, they were in her hotel room, naked on her bed.

Samantha was a blonde in her thirties, with full rounded breasts and a butt that made it difficult—she said—to find clothes that fit her well. There were times—she complained to him—that she knew she looked overweight.

"You sure don't look overweight now," he said, eyeing her naked form. "You look . . . perfect."

"That's because you like your women with some extra flesh on their bones," she said, slapping her own butt. "And I've got it."

He was across the room pouring two glasses of champagne. Now he walked to the bed and handed her a glass, then put his hand on her naked butt.

"Again," he said, "you're getting no complaints from me."

She smiled, transforming her face from lovely to beautiful. Her upper and lower lips were of equal fullness, which greatly appealed to him. It was one of the first things he noticed about her from across the room—that, and her breasts. In point of fact, she had caught the attention of most of the male diners in the restaurant, but she looked directly across the room, right back at him. There might as well have been no one else there.

Now they drank champagne and eyed each other's body. It was their third night together and they were still seeing things they hadn't noticed before.

A mole on her hip.

A bullet scar on his shoulder.

Another on his hip.

She leaned over and kissed his shoulder.

"That must've hurt," she said.

"They all hurt."

She touched the scar on his hip.

"All?" she asked. "Jesus, how many times have you been shot, honey?"

"I've stopped counting."

"That must be troublesome," she said, "always expecting someone to shoot at you."

"I was going to say, you get used to it. But now that I think about it, it *is* a hard way to live."

"Then why keep living that way?" she asked.

"Wherever I go, whatever I do," Clint said, "they'll follow me."

"Why not go somewhere and change your name?"

"You've heard about teaching old dogs new tricks?"

"Yes," she said, "you can't."

"Exactly."

"Well then," she said, putting her champagne glass down on a night table by the bed, "maybe you'd like to show me some of your old tricks?"

She reached into his lap to lovingly stroke his growing penis.

He put his glass down, then reached out to run his fingers over her breasts and nipples.

"Well, I think that can be arranged."

Her nipples reacted to his touch immediately, just as his penis did to hers.

She tugged on his cock while he leaned forward to kiss and bite her, and, when he was fully hard, she ducked her head and took him into her hot mouth. While she sucked him, he ran his hands over the smooth flesh of her back, down to her soft butt cheeks. Then he probed between her thighs from behind and got his middle finger up and into her and wiggled it. She gasped, but kept right on going until he was almost ready to explode. That's when she released his dick—hard, red, slick from her saliva—and moved around onto his lap and took him inside her hot, steamy cunt. She started bouncing up and down energetically on him and this time she didn't stop until he exploded inside of her . . .

***

Later he was down between her thighs, his face pressed to her crotch, his tongue probing through her blonde pubic patch until he found her, wet and waiting. She put her hands on the back of his head, in case he was thinking about moving, but he wasn't. He kept his tongue going until he felt her body tense, and then as waves of pleasure coursed through her, he climbed atop her and drove his hardness right into her . . .

And the night went on from there . . .

Chapter Two

Clint entered the Denver House Hotel on shaky legs, after another full night with Samantha, and headed for the stairs. As he moved past the front desk, the clerk called out to him. He changed direction and, when he reached the desk, he leaned heavily on it with both arms.

"I have a telegram for you, sir," the clerk said, holding it out to him.

"Thanks," Clint said, accepting it. "When did it come in?"

"Yesterday afternoon, after you had left."

"Your name's Baxter, right?"

"Yes, sir," the young clerk said, pleased that Clint had remembered.   He had been told by the manager that Clint Adams was an old and valued guest, and that no request from him was too great.

"Well, Baxter, would you have somebody bring some ham-and-eggs and coffee to my room? I don't think I'm going to be able to get back down here for breakfast once I make it to my room."

"Why, yes, sir," Baxter said, "I'll have one of the bellboys get to that right away."

"Thank you," Clint said. He handed the young man a dollar tip, then pushed away from the desk and continued his walk to the stairs.

***

Clint was in no hurry to read the telegram, because no matter what it said, he wasn't leaving his room for a while. So he washed up, changed his clothes, and admitted the bellboy with his breakfast, which he set down on a desk by the window.

The Denver House was one of the only hotels where Clint had a room overlooking the main street. Still, he never sat in front of the window, as there were a couple of buildings across the way from which a gunman could take a shot. Usually, upon his arrival, he moved the desk, so he could sit at it and not be a target in the window.

He sat, started on his breakfast, and only then did he read the telegram. It had been forwarded to him from Labyrinth, Texas by his friend, Rick Hartman, but the original sender was Jim West, from Washington D.C. Along with Rick Hartman, Bat Masterson, Wyatt Earp and Talbot Roper, West rounded out the five men Clint considered to be his good and close friends.

Jim West was never shy about drafting his friend Clint into the service of the government. And Clint was in the habit of never saying no to West. So when the telegram asked him to come to Washington on an urgent matter, he got on the earliest train, after sending Samantha an apologetic note, explaining that something had come up requiring his attention. But he promised he would be back in Denver soon. His intention was to return to see Roper, but at the same time to see her. In fact, as long as she lived in Denver, his visits from now on would be twofold.

But, for the foreseeable future, it was on to Washington . . .

***

The telegram told him to check into the Charter House Hotel, where there would be a suite waiting for him. It also told him that a soldier would be there to fetch him and take him to a meeting. West, as usual, would be on another assignment. Clint couldn't remember the last time he had actually seen James West, but that didn't affect his ability to do the man favors.

The morning after he arrived, there was a knock on the door and a Corporal saluted him and said he was there to transport him to the meeting. Out in front was a hansom cab, being pulled by two horses, which took them to a building where Clint would be meeting General George Hammond . . .

Chapter Three

"Sir," the Corporal said when he opened the door, "Mr. Clint Adams. Mr. Adams, General George Hammond." The Corporal withdrew and closed the door.

Clint entered and was surprised to find that it was simply a sitting room, replete with tables, chairs, and a sofa, like any hotel. Only this wasn't a hotel. Neither was it the building he usually met with the head of the Secret Service in.

"The Secret Service is moving up," he said, shaking hands with the bald, portly man in his fifties. The general looked to be in his dress uniform, complete with medals. There were two stars on each collar.

"Thanks for coming, Mr. Adams," Hammond said. "Have a seat." They both took a chair at the table, across from each other. "I'm not with the Secret Service. I'm with the Department of Indian Affairs."

And that was when he asked Clint if he had ever been to Florida, and mentioned Geronimo . . .

***

"Geronimo is in prison," Clint said.

"That's correct," Hammond said. "In Fort Pickens, on Santa Rosa Island in the Pensacola, Florida area."

"So as far from New Mexico and Arizona as you could put him," Clint said.

"He and his Apaches were captured in Mexico, but yet, his wife and children were sent to Fort Marion, in St. Augustine."

"Why?" Clint asked.

"It was decided that the braves—the warriors—should be kept separated from the women and children."

"It was decided. By you?"

"I was part of the team who made the decision, yes," Hammond said.

"But you didn't totally agree with it, did you?"

Hammond smiled. "No. How did you know that?"

"It was just . . . a feeling. I mean, from your attitude," Clint explained.

Hammond squared his shoulders.

"I wasn't aware I was betraying any . . . attitude."

"Well," Clint said, "suppose you just tell me what I'm doing here?"

"I told you," Hammond said. "Geronimo wants to see you."

"I've never met the man," Clint said. "Why would he want to see me?"

"He didn't say," Hammond replied. "He only says he wants to see you."

"In Florida."

"Well," Hammond said, "we don't want to take him out of the prison. We'd rather you go in to see him."

"But why?" Clint asked.

"Why what?"

"Why would you grant him the right to see me?"

"He may be a prisoner," Hammond said, "but he's still Geronimo. He has to be respected."

"I'll bet he's been asking to see his family," Clint said. "Why hasn't that request been respected?"

"As you said," Hammond answered, "I don't agree with every decision that's been made."

"And the people you don't agree with," Clint asked, "do they know you've sent for me?"

"No. I asked Jim West to aid me in contacting you, but nobody else knows."

"Except the Corporal who brought me here."

"He's been sworn to secrecy," Hammond said. "I trust him."

"So okay," Clint said, "that means I need to get myself to Pensacola, doesn't it? If I agree to go."

"I can make arrangements for you," Hammond said.

"But on the sly, right?"

"That's correct."

"So you're going to be in trouble if word gets out that you're doing this, right?"

"What I'm doing would probably keep me from ever earning another star," Hammond said, "and it might even cost me the ones I have."

"Well then," Clint said, "why don't you just let me get myself to Pensacola?"

"Very well," Hammond said, "but when you arrive, I'll have to get you in to see Geronimo."

"Why don't we worry about that when the time comes," Clint said.

"Then you'll go?"

Clint nodded.

"I'll leave in the morning."

General Hammond took a brown envelope from his pocket and slid it across the table.

"Expense money, and a train ticket."

Clint picked it up.

"You knew I'd agree?"

Hammond smiled.

"Jim West told me you would," he said.

"I've got to stop being so predictable," Clint said.

Chapter Four

The Corporal took Clint back to the hotel in the same hansom cab, which was a civilian vehicle. What Clint didn't know was, why the Corporal was in uniform?

"Corporal," he said, as the man stepped down, "you want to get a drink?"

"Sir?"

"I'm offering to buy you a drink," Clint said.

"In there?"

"They've got a bar in there, don't they?"

"I guess."

"Then why not come on inside and have a drink with me," Clint said.

"I don't know if I can."

"Do you have orders to the contrary?"

"Well, no . . ."

"Do you have orders to take me where I want to go?" Clint asked.

"Well, yes . . ."

"And right now," Clint said, "I want to go to the bar in this hotel."

The Corporal shrugged and said, "Oh, why not?"

They left the hansom right where it was and went inside. It was a short walk through the ornate lobby to the door that led to the bar. There were plenty of tables available, as the Washingtonians had not yet left their offices to start drinking, but Clint chose to simply stand at the bar. He thought that would make for a lighter atmosphere.

"Beer?" he asked the Corporal.

"Sure."

"Two beers," Clint told the bartender. "What's your name, Corporal?"

"O'Riley," the young man said. "Corporal Max O'Riley."

"Well, Max . . . can I call you Max?"

"Why not?" the young man asked. "You're buyin' the drinks."

The bartender put the two beers on the bar. Clint picked one up and handed it to the soldier.

"So," he said, "tell me about the General."

"Whataya wanna know?" the Corporal asked.

"Well," Clint said, "he seems to trust you. Why is that?"

"Mostly," the Corporal said, "it's because I don't talk about him."

Clint grinned.

"Good point," he said. "Do you know what job the General asked me to do?"

"No," the Corporal said. "All I know is I was supposed to pick you up, take you to see him, and bring you back. Oh, and not talk to anybody." He drained the beer, put the mug down. "And that includes you. Thanks for the drink."

Corporal O'Riley turned and left. Clint wondered if he would be back in the morning to take him to the train station, or if he would be on his own?

"Another one, sir?" the bartender asked.

"Hmm?" Clint looked down, realized he was holding an empty glass. "Oh, no, thanks." He dropped some money on the bar.

"Thank you, sir."

"Does the restaurant here in the hotel serve a good steak?" he asked the man.

The bartender thought a moment, then said, "Probably the second or third best in town, sir."

Clint decided the convenience was worth having the third best steak in town, and not go looking for the first or second.

"Thanks," Clint said. "I'll come back in for another drink after I eat."

"Yes, sir."

Clint left, reentered the lobby, then looked around for the entrance to the dining room. He spotted it right across from him and walked to it.

"Sir?" A man in a tuxedo greeted him. "Are you a guest?"

"Yes, I am."

"Room number?"

"Two-oh-seven."

"Would you like your meal to be added to your hotel bill?" the man asked.

"That would be great."

"Excellent," the man said. "Are you dining alone?"

"Yep. Just me."

"This way."

The dining room was half full. They worked their way through the maze of tables until they reached a table for two in the rear.

"Is this suitable?"

"Yes, it's fine," Clint said.

"Walter will be your waiter."

"Thank you."

Clint sat and waited for Walter. He didn't have long to wait.

"Sir?" A white-haired man in his sixties appeared at his table. "Can I get you something to drink?"

"I'll have a pot of coffee with a steak dinner."

"Excellent choice," Walter said. "We're quite well known for our steak."

"That's what I heard."

"It won't be long, sir."

The waiter turned and walked to the kitchen. At that moment, a man appeared at the entrance, looked around, saw Clint and walked to his table.

"Hello, Clint," Jeremy Pike said.

"Jeremy," Clint said. "What a coincidence."

"It's not a coincidence," Jeremy said. "Mind if I sit?"

"No, of course not," Clint said. "Join me."

The Secret Service Agent sat.

Chapter Five

Pike was in his forties, a sometime partner of Jim West's who Clint had worked with before. He considered the man a friend, though not on a level with West. He was dressed for work, in an expensive suit and shiny shoes.

"You want a steak?" Clint asked.

"You know what? Sure, why not?" Pike said. "Since I'm here."

Clint waved until Walter came over.

"Bring my friend the same thing I'm having," he said.

"Yes, sir."

"Lots of onions," Pike said.

"On both," Clint added.

"Yes, sir."

"Okay," Clint said, "so this isn't a coincidence. How did you know I was here?"

"Come on," Pike said. "I'm in the Secret Service, right?"

"Right," Clint said. "Eyes and ears everywhere."

"Exactly."

"Okay, let's move on," Clint said. "Why are you here?"

"I heard you were takin' a trip," Pike said.

"Is that right? What'd you hear?"

"That you're going to Florida."

"Who'd you hear that from?"

"You know," Pike said, waving his hand. "Ears."

"Right."

Walter came over to the table with two steak dinners, set them down.

"Good appetite, gents."

"Thank you, Walter."

Clint and Pike took a few moments to cut into their steaks and chew a few bites.

"Not bad," Pike said.

"Supposed to be third best in town," Clint said.

"Really?" Pike asked. "I know Morton's is better, but this tastes like a good second."

"I was told second or third best."

Pike pointed at Clint with a piece of steak on his fork and said, "Let's go with second."

"Deal," Clint said. "Pike, get to the point."

"Okay." Pike put his fork down, placed his hands together and leaned his chin on them. "You're going to Pensacola. And then you're probably going to St. Augustine."

"Why would I go to St. Augustine?"

"Because after Fort Pickens, I think you're going to have to go to Fort Marion." He waved both hands. "Somethin' to do with Geronimo's wife."

"Why are you worried about Geronimo's wife?" Clint asked, continuing to eat.

"I'm not," Pike said. "We'd like you to do us a favor while you're in St. Augustine."

"We?"

"The Secret Service."

"Ah."

"There's a man down there we'd like you to stop in and see," Pike said.

"And the man has a name?"

"He does."

"Are you going to tell me what it is?"

Pike picked up his knife and fork again.

"Only if you agree that you'll do it."

"Is that the way this is going to work?" Clint asked. "I thought maybe you'd tell me the name and then I'd decide whether or not I'd do it."

"You're not gonna know the name," Pike said.

"Then tell me," Clint said.

"He's a fella named Pelican Pete Davis."

"Pelican?"

"He's a boat captain," Pike said, "and he's brought somethin' in from Cuba that we need to pick up."

"Sounds like the kind of thing you or West do."

"It usually is, but we've got a lot goin' on right now," Pike said. "Jim's off on somethin', so's Artie Gordon and Frank Harper."

"And you?"

"One of us has to be here," Pike said.

"Is this why Jim 'volunteered' me for this job?"

"He didn't put your name up for anythin'," Pike said, "but when he heard they wanted you, he volunteered to be the go-between."

"So, if I'm doing one job, I might as well do the other," Clint said.

"Favors," Pike said, "let's call them favors, for your country."

"Okay," Clint said, "let's call them favors."

"So, will you do it?"

"Meet with your Pelican Pete?" Clint asked. "Sure, why not?"

"He'll be in St. Augustine, around the fort," Pike said. "But not in the fort, hopefully."

"Not a prisoner, you mean."

"Definitely," Pike said. "If he's a prisoner we're gonna be out of luck."

"What are the chances?"

"Well," Pike said, pushing his plate away, "he's kind of a smuggler, so . . ."

"So I go down there, and we hope for the best, huh?"

21

"That's about the size of it." Pike pushed his chair back. "I've gotta go. Thanks for the meal."

"It's not on you?" Clint asked.

"Isn't the government picking up your tab, here?" Pike asked.

"Yes, they are."

Pike smiled. "Then it's on me, isn't it?"

Chapter Six

The next morning, Corporal O'Riley knocked on Clint's door just as he was about to leave.

"I didn't know if you were taking me to the train station or not," Clint said.

"Those are my orders, sir."

"After breakfast?"

"That's your call, sir."

"O'Riley, drop the sir, okay?" Clint said. "I'm not in the army."

"Yes, si—um, okay."

"Let's go down. I'll check out, we'll have breakfast, and then you can drop me off."

"Right."

After having supper with Jeremy Pike, Clint wondered if he would have anymore surprise visitors before he left Washington?

***

After breakfast, they went out to the hansom cab in front of the hotel. Clint had one carpetbag with him, which he tossed into the back before climbing in himself.

"Do you need anything else?" the Corporal asked.

"No," Clint said. "Whatever else I need I'll be able to find when I get to Florida."

"Florida," Corporal O'Riley said. "That sounds so foreign. I've never been any further south than right here."

"Have you been west?" Clint asked.

"Oh sure," the Corporal said. "I've been as far west as Texas."

They stopped talking so that O'Riley could drive the cab to the train station. When they got there, he walked inside with Clint, accompanied him right to the train.

"This'll take you to Pensacola," he explained. "There won't be any need for you to change trains. Then you'll be able to take any other sort of transport to other parts of Florida. What about your own horse?"

"I left him in good hands in Denver," Clint said. "I'll be going back there when I'm done with these favors."

"Favors?"

Clint realized that O'Riley didn't know about his conversation with Jeremy Pike.

"I assume when I get there, I'll be asked to do something else," he said, and O'Riley accepted that.

"Do you have your ticket?" the soldier asked.

"Yes."

"Then you better get on board," O'Riley said. "I'll stay here until your train leaves."

Clint looked up and down the platform and saw a face he knew.

"You know what, kid? Get going. I'll be fine."

"Are you sure?"

"Yes," Clint said. "You got me here, you did your job. I'm on my own now. I'll make sure the General knows you did your job."

"Okay, then," O'Riley said. "Good luck."

They shook hands and the Corporal walked away. As soon as he disappeared, Clint saw the man coming toward him.

"Frank Harper," he said.

"Clint."

The two men shook hands.

"What are you doing here?" Clint asked. "I thought you were on assignment. I mean, that's what Pike said."

"Pike was right," Harper said. He was a tall, slender man in his forties, with dark hair and a dark mustache. "I just got back, and heard you were leavin' this mornin'. Thought I'd catch you here."

"Well, you did," Clint said. "What's going on, Frank?"

"I just wanted to warn you," Harper said. "If you end up goin' to St. Augustine, you've got to watch out for that fella, Pete Davis."

"Pelican Pete?"

"Yeah, that's what they call him," Harper said. "Pelican Pete."

"Pike told me he's a smuggler."

"He's right about that," Harper said. "But if you deal with this Pelican, he won't be alone."

"What are you saying?"

"I'm tellin' you to watch your back," Harper said. "It isn't the Wild West, but there are still some hard cases down there."

"I know that, Frank," Clint said. "I've dealt with plenty of hard cases in New York, even here in Washington. They're everywhere."

"Yes, they are," Harper said. "I just didn't want you going down south thinkin' it would be a walk in the park."

"Frank," Clint said, "is there something else you want to tell me? Something General Hammond or Pike hasn't?"

"No, Clint," Harper said, looking up and down the platform. "I'm just tellin' you to be careful."

Before Clint could say anything, Harper was gone, and a man down the platform was yelling, "All aboard!"

Chapter Seven

Clint didn't have a sleeper car, so he found himself seated by a window. Luckily, the car wasn't full, so he had nobody next to him, or across from him and was able to put his feet up.

He watched the scenery go by for a while, but it was nothing like what he'd seen traveling west. Eventually, he just closed his eyes and slept fitfully, stirring whenever anyone passed by in the aisle.

The train stopped every so often to pick up passengers and let some off, but before long somebody sat next to him, and across from him, and he decided to go to the dining car.

When he got there, he was able to get a table to himself. He hoped it would stay that way.

"Sir?" A black waiter appeared. "What can I get you?"

"A pot of coffee," Clint said. "Strong."

"Yessuh. And somethin' with it?"

"You got pie?"

"Yessuh, we got apple and cherry and, I think, rhubarb."

"I'll have apple," Clint said. "Or cherry. No rhubarb. Never rhubarb. Bring whichever of the other two you've got."

"Yessuh."

The waiter returned with the coffee and a large piece of cherry pie.

"Are you going to eat all that yourself?"

Clint looked up at the woman who had stopped by his table and asked the question. She was tall, dark haired, in her thirties, wearing a dark green traveling suit, definitely a woman of the East, not the West.

"Excuse me?"

"That's a huge hunk of pie," she said. "It looks like you might need some help."

"Well," Clint said, "are you doing anything at the moment?"

"Me? No, I'm free."

"Then join me," Clint said. "Please."

"Well . . ." She seemed to give the invitation some thought. "Okay."

She sat across from him.

"I'll get another fork from the waiter," he said, waving. "How about some coffee?"

"That would be wonderful," she said. "And if they have apple pie, we could share a hunk of that, too."

"Sure thing."

The waiter came over and Clint ordered the apple pie and another cup for coffee. While they waited, he shared his cherry pie.

"What's your name?" he asked her.

"Lily," she said.

"I'm Clint. Where are you headed?"

"Pensacola."

"So am I."

"How nice," she said. "And here I thought there would be no one interesting on this entire ride."

The waiter came, poured Lily some coffee, then put the apple pie and another fork down for them.

"So Lily," he said, "I didn't see you in the passenger car. Where are you sitting?"

"I knew this fifteen-hour trip was going to take twenty-four," she said. "What with all the stops, passengers getting on and off, stops for water, and we've already had some delays . . . so I made sure I got a sleeper."

"Good thinking," Clint said.

"I thought so," she said, "especially when I saw the men on this train, and the way they were looking at me. I felt secure being in a sleeper, but then I got hungry. I hope you don't mind, but when I came in here and saw you, I just thought you were . . . safe."

"Safe?"

She nodded.

"All the other men make me feel uneasy."

"Well," he said, "I guess I don't mind looking safe."

"Oh, definitely. So which of these do you like better, the apple or the cherry?"

They decided he liked the cherry and she liked the apple, so they each took that one and finished it while continuing to talk.

Lily worked in fashion, which was why her clothes looked as if they were from France. He told her he was just going down to Florida because he had never been there before.

"But what do you do?" she asked. "You know, to make a living?"

"Well . . . sometimes I work for the government."

"Really? Are you, like, a soldier?"

"No," he said, "I'm an independent contractor."

Her eyebrows went up.

"Are you, like, a mercenary?"

"Well, I wouldn't say that."

"But . . . you're wearing a gun." She leaned over so she could see the gun on his hip.

"Yes," he said, "I'm always wearing a gun."

"Then I guess that's why I felt I'd be safe with you." She stood up. "Thank you so much for the coffee and pie, and the company. Can I leave some money?"

"No, don't be silly," he said. "I'll take care of it."

She leaned over, kissed him on the cheek, filling his nostrils with her scent, and then walked away.

Somehow, when she mentioned she was in the sleeper car, he had the idea they might end up in her compartment.

Chapter Eight

Lily had the trip figured very well. There were quite a few stops that seemed to go on forever, even to the point of passengers getting off to stretch their legs. If Clint had realized the trip would take so long, into the night, he might have insisted the government get him a compartment in the sleeper car.

At one point, after dark, he was sitting with his arms folded, trying to get some sleep, but with a man next to him and two across, he felt hemmed in. Also, all three men were snoring.

He finally decided to stop trying and opened his eyes, but there was nothing to see outside the window. Then, suddenly, the door at the end of the car opened and Lily came in. She walked down the aisle and stopped alongside Clint's seat. The other three men were asleep, with their legs blocking the way to the aisle.

"Excuse me, gentlemen," she said, loudly.

They all came awake, one with a huge snort that alerted others in the car. Most of them were watching when she reached across and grabbed Clint's hand.

"Mr. Adams needs to come with me," she said.

The men all straightened their legs and watched as she pulled Clint into the aisle.

"And he won't be back til morning," she told them.

She went back up the aisle, with Clint trailing behind her.

When they got to the sleeper car she said, "You looked like you could use a place to sleep."

"Definitely."

"Well," she said, "I have to warn you, there's only one bunk."

"Really?"

"Well, no, there are two," she said, "but I only want to use one. Understand?"

"I think so."

When they got to her compartment, she opened the door and let him go in first. It was small, with two bunks, an upper and a lower.

He watched her lock the door, and then turn back to him. She was wearing the same suit she'd worn in the dining car, but now she peeled the jacket off.

"I thought we'd use the lower bunk," she said, tossing the jacket aside.

"That's fine with me."

She started to unbutton her blouse, then simply tore it open so that the buttons went flying. When her breasts came into view he was impressed. They were larger than he had thought—not huge, but bigger. The rest of her was long and sleek.

33

"Do you need help getting undressed?" she asked.

"Huh? Oh, no," he said. "I've got it."

He peeled off his own shirt, sat on the lower bunk to take off his bots, and then slid off his trousers and shorts. By then she was naked and so ready he could smell her.

She leaped on him and began kissing him, while reaching down to grasp his already hard cock. He ran his hands down her back, and when he reached her ass, he took hold of each cheek, and then flipped her onto her back.

"Oh yes," she said, as he began to kiss his way down her long, lean body—lean except for large, solid breasts that she apparently dressed to hide. "That's it."

When he got down between her thighs, he began to kiss the warm flesh while sliding a finger into her hot depths.

"Oh God," she said, reaching down to grab his head, "this is better than the passenger car, isn't it?"

"Oh, yeah . . ." he said, as she pressed his face to her wetness. "And better than pie, right?"

He stuck his tongue out, tasted her, and said, "Better than apple *or* cherry!"

***

Later she managed to flip him over onto his back, slide down and take his cock fully into her mouth.

"Mmmm," she moaned, then released him and grinned. "You're right, better than apple or cherry." She opened her mouth and captured him again. This time she kept sucking, and caressing his testicles, until he felt like his whole body was going to explode.

She felt it, too, though, and released him, giving it one last lick on the head before she sat back on her heels.

"Wow," she said, "look at that thing. It's almost like it's alive."

He looked down at his cock, which was huge and red and throbbing.

"Are you going to just leave it like that?" he asked.

"Oh no," she said, "I intend to thoroughly enjoy it. Just lay back, baby."

He settled down on his back and she climbed atop him, rubbing her wet pussy over the length of him. She was hot and slick and kept it up until he was totally wet from her. Then reached down to hold his penis and shimmied down on it. Once he was fully inside her steamy depths, she began to bounce up and down on him. Luckily the upper bunk folded up into the wall, or she would have been banging her head against it.

But now she had the freedom to bounce as high and come down as hard as she wanted to . . .

35

Chapter Nine

Clint woke the next morning with Lily lying on his left shoulder. The door was locked, but he still reached out to be sure he could touch his gun, which was on the floor.

She shifted, tossed one arm across him so that her large breasts were crushed against him. He could feel the large nipples poking into his chest. He looked out the window, saw the sunlight but not much else as the scenery went flying by.

"How fast are we going?" she asked, with her face against his chest.

"Us? Or the train?" he asked.

She bit him and said, "The train, silly."

"I don't know," he said. "We could be going anywhere from forty to sixty miles an hour."

"Wow," she said. "I guess we should be getting there soon."

"I'd say," Clint said.

"So we better hurry," she said, sliding her hand down between his legs.

"To breakfast?" he asked.

She laughed and closed her hand around his hardness.

"I think you know what I mean . . ."

***

After sex one more time, they got dressed and walked to the dining car for breakfast.

"How soon before we get to Pensacola?" she asked the waiter when he brought their food.

"About an hour, ma'am," he said. "in fact, we wuz just about to stop servin' breakfast."

"We made it just in time," Clint said. "Thanks."

They started to eat their eggs.

"So what are you going to be doing when we get to Pensacola?" Lily asked him.

"I have to go someplace called Santa Rosa Island."

"What's there?"

"Fort Pickens," he said. "It's a prison."

"You're going to prison?"

"Not because I belong there," he said. "There's just somebody I have to talk to."

"Who?"

"Well, that I can't say," he replied.

"Oh, I'm sorry," she said. "Must be some top secret government thing, huh?"

"Could be," Clint said. "What are you going down there for? And, by the way, where from?"

"I live in Boston," she said. "I'm going down to Pensacola to see about some new fashions."

"New fashions? From where? Paris?"

"No, these are from Cuba."

"Is that right?"

"Yes, it is," she said.

"I didn't know Cuba was known for their ladies' fashions," he commented.

"Well, they're not," she said. "But by the time I'm finished, they just might be."

"I wish you luck," he said.

She pushed her plate away.

"I have to go and pack," she said. "I should be done just about the time we get in."

"I'll see you on the platform then," he said.

"Do you think we might see each other in Pensacola?" she asked.

"I don't know how long I'll be there," he said.

"Do you know where you'll be staying?" she asked, standing up.

"No idea," he said.

"Well, I'll be at the Oakbrook Hotel," she said. "Pretty nice place, I'm told. You might try it."

"I just might," he said.

She smiled.

"See you around, Mr. Adams."

***

Clint was back in his seat, looking out the window as the train pulled into Pensacola.

People began to collect their bags, started jamming up the aisles so that they were standing in line to get out. Clint decided to wait and let everybody else file out before he grabbed his own bag and stood.

"Thank you for ridin' with us, sir," the tall conductor said, as he got to the end of the car.

"Maybe you can help me with something," Clint said.

"I will if I can, sir."

"Is there a hotel on Santa Rosa Island?"

"Santa Rosa?" the man said. "Well, no, sir. There's some folks who live out there, and have been for a long time. But mostly there's just Fort Pickens. You know, the prison."

"Yeah, I know," Clint said. "What about hotels in Pensacola?"

"A few good ones."

"Like the Oakbrook."

"Yeah, that's good," the conductor said. "Also, the Conch and the Black Pearl."

"Which of those three would you stay at?" Clint asked.

"I'd probably pick the Oakbrook."

"Okay, thanks," Clint said, and stepped onto the platform.

Chapter Ten

Clint didn't see Lily anywhere on the platform and ended up out in front of the train station, looking for a horse drawn cab to take him to the Oakbrook Hotel.

"Ride, sir?"

He turned and saw a small boy.

"What's that?"

"Do you need a ride?"

"I do," Clint said.

"My brother's wagon is just around the corner," the boy said. He looked all of ten.

"Why doesn't he pull it around here?" Clint asked.

"They don't allow him to do that," he said. "They're always chasin' us away."

Clint looked around, saw that by letting everyone else get off the train ahead of him, he had also missed out on most of the transportation.

"What's your name?" he asked.

"Kenny."

"Okay, Kenny," Clint said, "take me to your brother's wagon."

The boy smiled broadly.

"This way, sir."

He followed the boy around to the side of the train station, where another boy of about fifteen was waiting with a buckboard.

"This is your wagon?" Clint asked. "I was expecting a buggy of some sort."

"Sometimes we get people with lots of luggage," the older boy said. "That all you got?"

"Yes," Clint said. "Just this one bag."

"Well then," the boy said, "you can toss it in the back and ride up here with me."

"This is my brother, Danny," Kenny said.

"And where will you ride?" Clint asked Kenny.

"In the back, with your bag," Kenny said. "I ride back there all the time."

Clint did as he was told, tossed the bag into the bed of the buckboard, then climbed up and sat next to Danny.

"Where are you goin'?" Danny asked.

"The Oakbrook Hotel."

Danny made a face.

"Something wrong?" Clint asked. "I was told it was a good place to stay."

"Yeah," Danny said, "I guess. If you like fancy."

"I'll make do with it," Clint assured him.

***

It wasn't a long ride and soon they pulled up in front of the Oakbrook Hotel. Behind the building Clint saw a beach leading down to the water.

Clint dropped down and reclaimed his bag from the back.

"How much do I owe you?" he asked Danny.

"You can pay me what you want," Danny said.

"That's how we do it," Kenny explained, happily.

"Can I give you each something?"

"Sure, why not?" Danny asked.

He handed Danny a dollar, and then gave Kenny two bits.

"Thanks, Mister!" Kenny said.

"Thank you both," Clint said.

"Do you need a ride anywhere else while you're here?" Danny asked.

"Actually, I might," Clint said. "I've got to go to Santa Rosa Island."

"Do you know somebody who lives there?" Danny asked.

"No."

"Then you're goin' to the prison?"

"I am."

"When?"

"I'm not sure," Clint said. "I'll want to get the lay of the land here, so I'll probably go over there tomorrow morning."

"We can come back," Danny said. "If you want."

"That'd be fine," Clint said. "I'll see you both here in the morning."

"Thanks, Mister."

As the two boys climbed back up onto the buckboard Clint asked, "Do you two have any family? Parents?"

"Our parents are dead," Danny said. "It's just the two of us."

"You take care of Kenny?" Clint asked.

"We take care of each other!" Kenny spoke up.

"I see," Clint said. "Well, when you come back tomorrow morning, why don't you both have breakfast with me?"

"In there?" Danny asked, pointing at the hotel.

"I assume they serve breakfast."

"Yeah, to their guests," Danny said.

"And, I'm sure, to guests of their guests," Clint said.

"Can we, Danny?" Kenny asked, his eyes shining.

Kenny thought a moment, then asked, "Why?"

"You fellas might be able to answer some questions for me," Clint said. "I'll pay you by buying you breakfast. How's that sound?"

"Dann—" Kenny started, but the older boy cut him off with a wave of his hand.

"Okay," Danny said, finally, "we'll be here."

"Good," Clint said. "See you then."

He watched as the boys rode away in their rickety buckboard, then turned and walked to the hotel door.

Chapter Eleven

As Clint entered the hotel lobby, he saw what Danny meant by fancy. The floors were shiny-colorful tiles, and there were flowers all around him. He walked to the front desk and set down his bag.

"Welcome to the Oakbrook, sir," the clerk said. He was a dandy in his forties, well-dressed with every hair in place.

"I'd like a room, please," Clint said.

"Of course, sir," the clerk said. "Please sign the register."

Clint signed his name in the book, and wrote next to it: Labyrinth, Texas. The clerk turned the book around and read the name.

"That's odd," he said.

"What is?" Clint asked.

"Well, your name, Clint Adams," the clerk said. "There's a legend out West of a man by that name. They call him the Gunsmith."

"How do you know about him?" Clint asked.

"I read," the clerk said. He reached under the desk and came out with a dime novel. TALES OF THE GUNSMITH was the title. It was one of those things that Clint never read.

"What do you know about that?" Clint said. "Can I have my key?"

"Of course, sir," the clerk said. "A room overlooking the front?"

"No," Clint said, "something along the side would be good."

"There you go," the clerk said, handing him a key. "Do you need help—"

"No, I just have this," Clint said. "Thanks."

He went up the stairs to the second floor of the three story hotel. He was happy to see that there was no elevator. He entered his room, found the same flowery décor that existed in the lobby. It was almost too bright, but he figured he would get used to it.

He took the two extra shirts he had from his bag and hung them in the closet. His extra underwear he put in a drawer. He wasn't used to being in hotels without his saddlebags and rifle. The only other thing he had was a book, Mary Shelley's FRANKENSTEIN. He put it on the night table next to the large four poster bed.

He walked to the window and looked out, was satisfied that it overlooked a side street with nothing across from it, and no access from outside.

He decided to go and take a walk. As he had told the boys, he wanted to get the lay of the land. He went back downstairs, through the lobby and out the front. There were buildings in both directions, so he simply picked left and started walking.

Every step he took was accompanied by the sound of the water as it washed over the shore. He had seen oceans before, on both coasts, had travelled by boat to England and South America. The ocean didn't hold any real interest for him, so he wasn't drawn to the beach. Instead, he walked past shop after shop, and when he saw one that sold men's clothes, he went inside and bought another pair of trousers. He didn't know how long he would be in Florida, so he also bought a couple of new shirts.

When he was done walking one side of the street, he crossed over to the other, started working his way back to the hotel. He ignored the side streets. Before reaching the hotel, he passed a small restaurant that also had a bar, went inside for some lunch. The waiter told him a popular menu item was clams, so he ordered some. When they came, he had some difficulty, so the young waiter showed him how to open them, and he went from there. They satisfied his hunger, but clams were not something he thought he would ever eat again.

"Have you lived here all your life?" he asked the young man.

"Yes, sir."

"How far are we from Santa Rosa Island?"

"A few miles," the young man said, "but that's not someplace you wanna go, sir. There are a few old timers still living out there in old cottages, but the main part of the island is taken up by Fort Pickens. That's a prison, sir."

"I see."

"Besides," the waiter went on, "they wouldn't let you near there, not unless you were maybe visiting a prisoner."

"Thanks for telling me that . . . what's your name?"

"Sandy."

"Thanks, Sandy."

Clint paid his bill and added a generous tip for Sandy.

***

The hotel had a large front porch with chairs, so Clint decided to spend the early evening sitting out there, enjoying the breeze that came in off the ocean. He was glad it was March, because he knew it could get very hot in Florida in the summer. He was used to Southwest hot, but as he understood it, Florida hot was also humid.

But for the moment, he closed his eyes and smelled the sea breeze. Maybe a walk down to the beach wouldn't be bad after all. But before he could do that, he smelled something else familiar.

"Hi, cowboy."

He looked up and saw Lily.

"How'd you find me?" he asked.

"I just walked out the front door and here you are," she said, with a smile.

"That's right, you said you were staying here," he said.

"It *is* the nicest place in town, right?"

"I suppose."

"Well, judging from my room," she said, reaching down to take his hand. "You want to see it?"

"Sure."

She drew him to his feet, and he followed her into the hotel . . .

***

Her room was identical to his, but that really wasn't the point. They undressed as soon as they entered and tumbled onto the bed. It was nice to have more room than they'd had in her compartment.

She sat astride him with his cock buried inside her. Her hands pressed flat to his chest.

"Am I keeping you from something important?" she asked.

"Not a thing," he said, putting his hands on her breasts. "I have nothing to do until tomorrow."

"Then we have all night?"

"We do."

She laughed and began to bounce up and down on him faster and faster.

"This is going to be fun," she moaned. "A real bed, a real room, and time."

"Only one thing," he said.

"What's that?"

He quickly flipped her over, bringing a cry of surprise from her.

"You're not in control," he said. "I am."

He was still inside of her, and started plunging in and out, quickly.

"That's okay with me," she said, her eyes wide. "Oh, God . . ."

***

In the morning Lily rolled over and kissed his bare chest until he woke.

"I've got work to do today," she said.

"So do I," he said.

"How long will it take you?" she asked.

"Most of the day, I expect."

"Me, too," she said. "In fact, I don't know that I'll have any more time for . . . this." She slid her hand down between his legs.

"Are you saying what I think you're saying?" he asked.

"What else would I be saying?" she asked, slithering down to take his hardening cock into her mouth. "This might be our last time together, so let's make it worth it."

***

"We can't have breakfast together," she said, as they got dressed. "I've got a meeting."

"So have I," he said.

"So I guess we'll just have to see if we run into each other again while we're here."

"I'm going to be moving on to St. Augustine," he said.

"And I'm going to be heading back north," she said. "If you ever get up that way . . ."

"I'll keep it in mind," he promised.

Chapter Twelve

He was waiting out on the porch when the two boys pulled up in their buckboard. Kenny ran up onto the porch, but Danny just walked, not wanting to seem too anxious.

Clint took them into the lobby and to the hotel dining room.

The other diners, all hotel guests, stared as he walked the boys to a table.

"Sir," the waiter said, rushing over to the table, "are you a guest?"

"Yes, I am," Clint said, "and these boys are my guests. Understand?"

"Oh, yes, sir," the diminutive waiter said. He was bald, with watery, nervous eyes. "What can I get you?"

"Steak-and-eggs, boys?"

"Yeah!" Kenny said, eagerly

"Sounds good," Danny said.

"Three steak-and-egg breakfasts. Coffee for me, and milk for the boys."

"Coffee for me," Danny said.

"Me, too!" Kenny spoke up.

"Milk for the boys," Clint repeated.

"Yes, sir, comin' right up," the waiter said.

"Milk?" Danny asked.

"I'm paying, right?" Clint asked. "Milk."

When the breakfasts came, the boys tucked into it and didn't seem to object to washing it down with milk. Clint could not keep up with them. By the time they finished, he was only half done.

"You guys want to split what I have left?" he asked. "I'm pretty full."

"Sure!" Kenny said.

Clint portioned out the meat, eggs and potatoes he had left onto each boy's plate and sat back to drink coffee while he watched them eat.

When they both finished and pushed their empty plates away, Clint asked, "You boys have enough?"

"Oh, yeah, it was great!" Kenny said, enthusiastically.

"Danny?"

"I had enough."

"How was it?"

Danny shrugged.

"Okay."

"Well, I'm glad you boys are happy."

"What now?" Danny asked. "You still goin' to the prison?"

"I am. How do I get there?"

"There's a ferry goes over," Danny said. "We can take you there."

"Good."

"But when you get there, you're gonna need a real good reason for them to let you in."

"I think I've got one."

"Well, okay then," Danny said. "Let's get movin'. We've got other things to do today."

"No, we ain't, Danny—"

"Quiet, Kenny!" Danny said, standing up. "You ready to go, Mister?"

"Clint, you boys can just call me Clint, and yes, I'm ready to go."

***

Danny pulled the buckboard to a stop in front of a dock that was empty, at the moment.

"The ferry'll be here before long," Danny told him.

"Thanks, boys," Clint said, dropping down to the ground.

"You gonna need a ride back?" Danny asked, as Clint handed him a few dollars.

"I will," Clint said, "but I'm not sure when."

"Well," Danny said, "the ferry runs every two hours. We'll just keep checkin' back to see if you're on it."

"I'd appreciate that, boys," Clint said. "Thanks."

"See ya later, Clint!" Kenny yelled.

Clint waved as the boys drove off, then turned to wait for the ferry.

***

When Clint disembarked on the island, he asked the pilot if it was true the ferry ran every two hours.

"Give or take," the old man said.

"Give or take what?" Clint asked.

"I been known to fall asleep and be a little late," the pilot admitted.

"Okay," Clint said, "but nearly every two hours, right?"

"Right."

"Thanks."

"You, uh, going to the fort?" the pilot asked.

"I am."

The man pointed.

"Take that path. Leads right to the front gate."

"Thanks."

The pilot nodded and waved.

As he walked the path, he thought about the other people who had been on the ferry. There were only a few, and they all seemed to be those "old timers" he was told still lived on the island. They didn't talk to him and, he noticed, they also didn't speak to each other. They appeared to be people who liked keeping to themselves.

He walked for about fifteen minutes before he came to a curve in the road which revealed the fort ahead of him. He hoped he was mere moments away from finding out what Geronimo, the most famous of all Indian chiefs, wanted with him.

Chapter Thirteen

He presented himself at the gate and was taken immediately to the office of the warden.

"Clint Adams?" the tall man behind the desk said. "Horace Watson." He came around with his hand out. "Happy to meet you."

They shook hands.

The warden looked past Clint at the guard who had accompanied him to the office and said, "That's all. Wait outside."

"Yes, sir."

The guard left, and the warden went back around his desk. He looked to be in his fifties. He was wearing a white shirt with the sleeves rolled up. There was a jacket hanging on the back of his chair.

"Can I offer you anything? Coffee, lemonade, bourbon?"

"None of those, thanks," Clint said. "I'm just here to see Geronimo."

"Yes, well," Watson said, "why don't we sit and talk first?"

"About what?"

"Please," Watson said, indicating the chair across from him. Clint finally relented and sat.

"Geronimo has not exactly been a model prisoner," Watson said.

"Uh-huh," Clint said. "He's kind of an old man, isn't he?"

"Not really," Watson said. "I mean, he's not sixty yet."

"But he's probably kind of . . . worn out."

"He's actually pretty robust," Watson said.

"So what are you trying to tell me?"

"When you talk to him," Watson said, "I'd like you to try to convince him to be more cooperative in the future."

"Maybe," Clint said, "if you allowed him to see his wife—"

"That's not my call," Watson said, interrupting him. "I'm just trying to keep things under control here."

"I see," Clint said. "Well, I guess I'm going to have to find out why he wants me here first. Then maybe I can do something for you."

"Fair enough." Watson stood. "Wait here, I'll have the chief brought to you."

"Thank you," Clint said. "I thought I'd have to talk to him in his cell."

"No," Watson said. "Here's fine."

"And could you bring us something to drink, maybe to eat?" Clint asked.

"Sure," Watson said. "I'll see to it."

The warden left his office.

Clint got up, walked to the window behind the desk. It looked down into a yard where some of the prisoners were milling about. From his vantage point, they didn't all look like Indians, but there were enough of Geronimo's Chiricahua Apaches there to cause trouble, if he wanted to. That was probably what the warden was talking about.

The door opened and two prison employees entered carrying trays. There was coffee and lemonade, as the warden had mentioned, but no bourbon. On the other tray was some bread and meats, the makings for sandwiches.

Both men simply nodded at Clint, put the trays down, and left.

Since Clint had given half his breakfast to the brothers, Kenny and Danny, he walked over, picked up a piece of meat and popped it into his mouth. It was beef, not bad, probably a lot better than what they normally fed the prisoners.

He was chewing on a second piece, this time turkey, when the door opened again.

"Clint Adams," Warden Watson said, as he entered, "this is Geronimo."

The Apache came in behind Watson, wearing shackles on his wrists and ankles. Somehow, Clint thought he would be bigger. His hair was long and gray, and his skin was dry and looked cracked. There were two armed guards behind him.

"Can we talk alone?" Clint asked.

"Sure," Watson said, nodding to the guards.

"And can we take those chains off?"

Watson stopped and looked at Clint.

"We'll take them off his wrists." He gestured to one of the guards. "But not his ankles."

"Okay."

One guard undid the wrist chains and then Watson and the two guards left.

Clint turned and looked at Geronimo. He had coffee colored eyes that were very clear as he stared back at him.

"Geronimo," Clint said, "it's an honor."

Geronimo looked at the food on the table.

"Let's sit," Clint said, "eat, drink, and talk."

Geronimo grunted and sat in the chair Clint had been using. Clint walked around and sat in the warden's chair.

"You are Clint Adams?" Geronimo asked, while chewing on a piece of beef. He ignored the bread.

"That's right." Clint did the same, snagged a piece of turkey and put it in his mouth.

"The Gunsmith," Geronimo said.

"Yes."

"I asked for the Gunsmith," Geronimo said.

"I know," Clint said, "that's why I'm here."

"We have never met."

"I know that, too," Clint said. "Why did you ask for me, then?"

"I have known of you for a long time," Geronimo said.

"From who?"

"Many who have seen you, and been impressed by you," Geronimo said. "Quanah Parker is one."

"You're Apache and Quanah is Comanche."

Geronimo stared at him and chewed on a piece of turkey.

"Okay, forget that," Clint said. "What did you want to see me about?"

"How do I know you are the Gunsmith?" Geronimo asked.

"Who else would I be?" Clint asked.

"Another lying white eyes," the Apache medicine man said.

"For what reason?"

Geronimo shrugged.

"Why do the whites need a reason to lie?" he questioned. "It has never been so before."

"Geronimo," Clint said, "I know you have been lied to by my people, but I am not here to lie to you. I am here because you asked for me."

"I need to know you are who you say you are," Geronimo said. "I need to know you are who I asked for."

"How do you propose I prove that?" Clint asked.

"With your weapon."

"I'm not going to fire my gun in here," Clint said. "Who knows what a panic that might cause. Unless that's what you want?"

"I will have to look into your eyes," Geronimo said, "and decide if I trust you."

"Do it, then," Clint said.

Geronimo didn't move, but his coffee-brown eyes suddenly became more intense as he stared at Clint. Then he reached for another piece of beef.

"I will believe you," he said.

"Good," Clint said, "then why am I here?"

Chapter Fourteen

"Now that I accept that you are Clint Adams," Geronimo said, "you are the only white man I will trust."

"I suppose I should be flattered," Clint said. "Trust me with what?"

"My family."

"They're in Fort Marion, right?" Clint asked. "In St. Augustine?"

"That is right," Geronimo said.

"How many children?"

"Three," Geronimo said. "Dohn-say, Fenton and Lenna."

"And your wife?"

"Three of my wives are there," Geronimo said.

"Three?" Clint asked.

Geronimo nodded. "Ih-tedda, Zi-yeh and She-gha."

"How many wives do you have?" Clint asked.

"Nine."

"Nine wives?" Clint asked, in disbelief.

"But only three are in Fort Marion."

"Okay," Clint said, "So what do you want from me?"

"My people are dying in Fort Marion," Geronimo said. "I want my wife and children to be brought here, before they die, too."

"And for this you thought of me?"

"Among my people you are known as an honorable man," Geronimo said. "An honorable white man. That is rare."

Clint wished he could argue with Geronimo on that.

"What do you expect me to do, Geronimo?"

"Get them out," the Apache said. "Save their lives. That is all I ask."

"What makes you think I have any power to do that?" Clint asked.

"I do not know if you do," Geronimo said, "but I know you are the only white man I can ask."

"You could've asked the President," Clint suggested.

"I do not trust him."

"You could've asked General Cook." Cook was the man who captured Geronimo.

"I do not trust him, either," Geronimo said. "I trust only you, the legendary Gunsmith."

"If I am, in fact, him," Clint reminded him.

The old Indian smiled at that.

"You are he," he said. "Of that I am now sure."

"Why?"

"I have looked into your eyes," Geronimo said, "and seen only truth."

Clint studied the man.

"Will you do it?" Geronimo asked.

J.R. Roberts

"I don't know if I can."

"Will you try?"

"Well," Clint said, "I've come all the way down here, so I suppose the least I could do is try."

"That is all I ask."

As if on cue, the door opened, and the warden entered with two guards.

"How are we doing?" Warden Watson asked.

"I think we're done," Clint said, "for now."

He saw Geronimo grab two hands full of beef and close his fists over them. One guard came over and shackled his wrists again.

"I will wait to hear from you," Geronimo said. "Thank you."

"Don't thank me yet," Clint said, as the Apache medicine man was led from the room.

"What did he have to say?" the warden asked.

"Quite a few things," Clint said, "but I'm afraid they're going to have to be between him and me."

"What?"

"I thought this prison would be run by a soldier," Clint said.

"It was," Watson said, "and probably will be again. I was brought in temporarily."

"Do you know who runs Fort Marion?"

"Yeah, Lieutenant Colonel Loomis L. Langdon. Why, is that where you're goin' next? Is that what Geronimo wanted?"

"I just have another job to do while I'm down here," Clint said. "Where the hell is St. Augustine, anyway?"

"Way down on the other side of Florida," Watson said. "You'll have to go through Jacksonville."

"Can I ride there?" Clint asked. "I've had enough of trains for a while."

"Sure. but it's about four hundred miles. Just head to Jacksonville, and, when you get there, head south. It's about forty miles from there."

"Okay, thanks."

As Clint headed for the door, Watson settled down behind his desk and started to make himself a sandwich.

"So you're really not gonna tell me what you and the Chief talked about?"

Clint turned at the door and looked back at the warden.

"Geronimo was never a chief," Clint said. "He's a medicine man."

"What the hell's the difference?" Watson said.

Clint shook his head and left.

Chapter Fifteen

When he took the ferry back to Pensacola, he found the boys Kenny and Danny, waiting for him.

"Did you get into the prison?" Kenny asked.

"I got in," Clint said, climbing up onto the seat next to him.

"Who'd ya see?" Danny asked, kneeling behind him.

Clint looked at the two boys' inquiring faces, and wondered, why not?

"Geronimo."

"For real?" Danny asked.

"You didn't see Geronimo," Kenny challenged.

"I did," Clint insisted.

"Why?"

"He asked for me."

"Geronimo asked for you?" Danny said, skeptically. "In person?"

"That's right."

"Why?"

"He wants a favor."

"Are ya gonna do it for him?" Danny asked.

"I'm going to try."

"Why would he ask for you?" Kenny inquired.

"Well, he says it's because I'm the only white man he can trust."

"Yeah, right," Kenny said.

"He's famous!" Danny said.

"I know he is."

"Are you famous?"

"Not as famous as he is," Clint said, although he didn't know if that was quite true.

"Whataya gonna do now?" Kenny asked.

"Well," Clint said, "I need a horse."

"What for?"

"I've got to ride to, uh, Jacksonville."

"That's a long ride," Kenny said. "Why don't ya take a train?"

"I'm tired of trains," Clint said. "You know where I can get a horse?"

"I know a guy—" Kenny started.

"Do you know where I can get a good horse?" Clint said, cutting him off.

Kenny thought a moment.

"Okay, yeah, I know somebody. You wanna go there now?"

"Yes, let's go now," Clint said, "and then I'll buy you boys supper."

"At your hotel?" Kenny asked.

"No," Clint said, "someplace you guys pick. Someplace you like."

"Wow," Kenny said. "Where should we go, Danny?"

"I dunno," Danny said, "I'll think about it."

***

Kenny drove Clint right to a large barn, with a big corral out in front. At the moment, though, the corral was empty.

"This is the place?" Clint asked.

"This is where I got my horse," Kenny said, indicating the broken-down, sway-backed nag that was pulling his buckboard.

"Is that a fact?"

"Yeah," Kenny said, "they was gonna put 'er down, but I took 'er."

"I see."

"Come on," Danny said, jumping down, "I'll introduce ya."

They walked to the barn with Kenny running behind them.

"You guys got a last name?" Clint asked.

"Yeah," Kenny said, "it's McBain."

"And no other relatives?"

"Nope," Kenny said. "It's just us."

"Where do you live?"

"We got a room," was all Danny would say.

The two large doors in front were closed, so Kenny took Clint around to the smaller door on the side. He knocked and it was almost immediately opened. The man standing there was large, in his late thirties, with a frown that turned into a smile when he saw Kenny and Danny.

"Hey, boys," he greeted.

"Hi, Jamie," Kenny yelled.

"Who's this?" Jamie asked, looking at Clint.

"He's our friend," Kenny said.

"His name is Clint," Danny said. "He needs to buy a horse."

"Or rent one," Clint said. "Hello." He stuck out his hand.

Jamie shook hands and said, "Come on in."

As they entered, Clint saw there were horses inside.

"I have six here," Jamie said. "Choose one and we'll negotiate a price for sale, or rent."

Clint walked to each of the stalls to inspect the animals. There were none there to match his own Darley Arabian, Eclipse, but he did find a mare who looked as if she was built for stamina.

"I have to ride to St. Augustine," he told Jamie.

"That'll take the better part of a week," Jamie said.

"This mare looks capable."

71

"She is," Jamie said. "She's six years old, and in fine fettle."

"Good," Clint said, "then let's work out a price."

"Come this way," Jamie said. "I have a small office in the back."

Clint followed him.

Chapter Sixteen

Kenny and Danny took Clint to a small café near the water, where the boys ordered both clams and shrimp. Clint skipped the clams, but enjoyed the shrimp.

"You worked out a good price with Jamie," Danny said.

"Did I? I just figured since I'd probably be coming back here, I should rent, not buy."

"When will you be comin' back?" Kenny asked.

"I'm not sure," Clint said. "That'll depend on how long it takes me to do the job."

"And what's the job?" Kenny asked.

"I'll actually find out when I get there."

"When are ya leavin'?" Kenny asked.

"Tomorrow morning."

Kenny looked sad. Clint knew what he was thinking. No more good meals.

"You know," Clint said, "you boys deserve a finder's fee."

"Finder's fee?" Danny asked.

"Yeah," Clint said, "you helped me get the horse. Plus, Jamie threw in a saddle."

"So what's a finder's fee?" Kenny asked.

"It means I give you some money for helping me," Clint said.

"But you still pay us for drivin' you, right?" Danny asked.

"Right."

"Then a finder's fee sounds good," Danny said. "How much?"

"How does twenty dollars sound?"

"Wow! Twenny?" Kenny yelled.

"Shhhh, Kenny," Danny said. "Keep it down." He looked at Clint. "When do we get it?"

"After you drop me at Jamie's in the morning," Clint said. "How's that sound?"

"It sounds good to me," Kenny said.

"Yeah," Danny said. "That's okay."

"Good," Clint said, "Let's finish eating and then you can take me back to my hotel."

"Can we get some more shrimp?" Kenny asked.

"Yes," Clint said, waving to the waiter, "more shrimp."

***

Danny pulled the buckboard to a stop in front of the hotel. Clint was about to step down from the seat when the shooting started. Somebody cried out in pain. He reached for the two boys and dragged them down to the ground. That was when he saw the blood on Danny.

As the shooting continued, he pulled both boys under the buckboard with him.

"Just lie still," he told them.

"What's happenin'?" Kenny asked.

"Just stay here!" Clint said.

"I—I think I'm shot," Danny moaned.

Clint rolled him over, saw the blood on his shoulder. By then the shooting had stopped. Clint knew if he left the boys there and tried to find the shooters, Danny might bleed out.

People were pouring out of the hotel to see what was happening. Clint looked across the street, from where he thought the shots had come, but didn't see anybody.

"Ow, it hurts," Danny whispered.

"Okay, kid," Clint said, "come on, we're going to get you to a doctor."

He crawled out from beneath the buckboard, pulled Danny out and picked him up.

"Come on, Kenny."

Carrying Danny, he ran inside the hotel lobby while the guests looked on.

"Is there a doctor here?" he yelled.

Chapter Seventeen

One of the guests was a doctor, who ran to his room for his bag. Clint laid Danny down on one of the sofa's in the lobby while the desk clerk complained about the blood.

"Shut up about the blood!" Clint shouted at him. "Get me a blanket."

"Yessir."

The doctor returned with his bag at the same time the clerk came back with a blanket.

"Get me some hot water," the doctor told him.

"Yessir."

"Is my brother gonna be okay?" Kenny asked.

"Just stand aside and let me take care of him, son," the portly doctor said, giving Clint a look.

"Come on, Kenny," Clint said. "Let's give the doctor some room." He pulled the boy off to one side as the clerk returned with a basin of water.

The doctor tore off Danny's shirt while a crowd gathered to watch.

"Ow, it hurts like hell!" Danny moaned.

"Take it easy, son," the doctor said. "You're going to be fine." The sawbones looked over his shoulder at Clint. "Why don't you get all these people back."

"Right. Come on, everybody. There's nothing to see, here. It's all over."

"Not quite," a voice said.

The crowd started to disperse and a man wearing a badge appeared. He was average height, in his early thirties, with an oddly shaped badge on his chest. He was well dressed in a clean shirt and trousers, but it wasn't a uniform.

"Are you the man who was with the boy when he was shot?"

"That's right."

He looked down at Kenny.

"And this is his brother?"

"Yes."

"Is that a doctor?"

"Yes."

"Doc, how's the boy?"

"He's going to be all right," the doctor said. "I just need to finish up."

"Then I can talk to him?"

"Sure."

He looked at Clint.

"Can we talk outside?"

"Sure, Sheriff," Clint said. "Or is it police—"

"I'm the local constable," the man said. "My name's Snyder."

"Constable Snyder," Clint said.

"Right. Can we go outside?"

"Sure." He looked down. "Kenny, why don't you stay—"

"No, the boy, too," Constable Snyder said. "He's a witness, right?"

"Right."

"This won't take long."

"Okay," Clint said. "Come on, Kenny."

"Will Danny be here when we come back?" Kenny asked.

"Yes, he'll be here."

The three of them stepped outside.

***

The constable had Clint recount what had happened, and then asked Kenny a bunch of questions about what he saw. When they were done, he stared off across the street.

"So, from there?" he asked, pointing.

"Yes, somewhere over there," Clint said.

"But you didn't see anyone?"

"No," Clint said, "I tried to get the boys under cover, and then I saw that Danny was hit. As people began to run out of the hotel, the shooters were gone."

"Shooters?" the constable said. "Are you sure there was more than one?"

"There were two."

"How could you tell?"

"I heard two guns," Clint said.

"And you know enough about guns to tell the difference?" the constable asked. "I mean, a gunshot is a gunshot, right?"

"Wrong," Clint said. "And yes, I know guns."

"How?"

"Constable," Clint said, "you haven't asked me my name."

Snyder, who had been writing on a pad of paper, looked up and said, "Yes, I know. I was getting to that." He wrote something else, then looked up. "And your name, sir?"

"Clint Adams."

"Clint . . . Adams?" The man studied him. "That's odd."

"What is?"

"Well, I read these books about a man named Clint Adams, from out West," Snyder said. "The Gunsmith? You ever heard of him?"

"Constable," Clint said, "I am him."

Now the constable dropped his arms to his side and stared.

"Wait," he said, "you're the Gunsmith?"

"Yes," Clint said. "That's how I know there were two shooters. And they were both using rifles."

"Can you prove you're the Gunsmith?"

"Well," Clint said, "I can shoot somebody, or you could go out to Fort Pickens and check with the warden. He'll vouch for me."

The constable wrote something else down. When he looked at Kenny, the boy was staring at Clint with wide eyes.

"And you didn't see anybody?" Snyder asked.

"No, sir," Kenny said. "I didn't see nobody."

"All right," the constable said. "How much longer were you planning on being here, Mr. Adams?"

"I'm leaving tomorrow," Clint said. "Is that okay?"

"Well," Snyder said, "I'll be askin' some more questions today. Why don't I check back with you in the morning?"

"Sure."

"Meantime," Snyder said, "one more question."

"What?"

"Do you think the shooters were after you, or the kids?" Snyder asked.

Clint stared at the man for a few seconds.

"Well," he said, "I assumed it was me, but now that you mention it, they were pretty bad shots if they were trying to hit me."

"I'll go inside and talk to the older boy."

"Okay," Clint said.

As the constable went inside Clint said to Kenny, "Come on, let's sit down here on the porch."

Chapter Eighteen

"Are you really the Gunsmith?" Kenny asked.

"I am," Clint said. "How do you know that name?"

"You *are* famous," Kenny said. "More famous than Geromino."

"That's Geroni-mo," Clint said. "You really think so?"

"Oh, yeah," Kenny said. "Wow, the Gunsmith."

"Kenny," Clint said, "why would someone shoot at you or Danny?"

"I dunno."

"Come on," Clint said, "what else does Danny do to get money for you guys? I mean, other than driving the buckboard."

"Well . . . sometimes he steals."

"Steals what?"

"Sometimes we steal food," Kenny said. "You know, apples, oranges, maybe bananas. But since you're gonna give us twenny dollars, we can buy that stuff."

"Yes, you can," Clint said.

Clint thought about it. There was no reason for anyone down here to shoot at him. He didn't think anyone would recognize him on the street. But then again, there *was* his meeting with Geronimo. What if somebody didn't like the idea? It would have to be someone from the prison. A guard. Maybe the warden, himself, sent someone after him.

But it happened too quickly. How could the word have gone out that soon? Was there a telegraph key at the fort?

The constable came back out, looked over at Clint, touched his hat and left. They would be seeing each other in the morning.

He was followed out by the doctor, who looked around, saw Clint and walked over.

"The boy was with you?"

"Yes," Clint said. "This is his brother."

"Is he the only relative?"

"Yes."

The portly man looked down at Kenny.

"Son, your brother's going to be all right. A little sore, but if he gets the rest he needs, he'll be fine. Can you see that he does that?"

"I—I don't know," Kenny said, honestly. He looked at Clint. "We take care of each other, but neither of us ain't never been shot before."

"I'll help you take him home," Clint said. "Can he be moved, Doc?"

"Yes," the doctor said. "The bullet dug a furrow along his shoulder. There was a lot of blood, but it kept going,

J.R. Roberts

so there's no permanent damage. I have a makeshift bandage on it for now." He looked at Kenny, again. "If you tell me where you live, I'll come by tomorrow, clean it again and bandage it properly."

"A-all right."

"Thank you, Doctor—"

"Thomas," the doctor said, "Henry Thomas."

Clint stood and shook hands with the man.

"I'm Clint Adams."

"You're a guest of the hotel, aren't you, Mr. Adams?"

"Yes, but I have to leave tomorrow."

"I have an idea . . ." the doctor said.

***

Clint carried Danny up to his hotel room and put him in the bed.

"Ain't this your room?" Kenny asked.

"It's yours now," Clint said, "yours and Danny's."

The doctor's idea was for Clint to give his room to the boys for a few days. Then the doctor could look in on Danny while Clint was away, clean and bandage the wound properly. He and his wife were going to be at the hotel til the end of the week. At that point, the doctor figured Danny could go home.

As far as paying for the room, since the boy was shot in front of the hotel, Clint and the doctor were able to convince the hotel manager to put the boys up for a week.

"You mean, we get to stay here?" Kenny asked.

"That's right," Clint said. "You can share the bed, and here's the finder's fee I promised you."

Kenny took the money and counted it.

"You said twenny dollars," he said. "This is fifty."

"You can have some meals brought up here for Danny, while he's recovering."

At the moment, Danny was asleep. Kenny looked over at his big brother.

"Is he really gonna be okay?"

"He's going to be fine," Clint assured him. "The doc seems to know what he's doing."

"Where you gonna sleep?" Kenny asked.

"I'll get another, smaller room just for tonight," Clint said.

"So you're still leavin' tomorrow?"

"I'm sorry, Kenny, but I have to," Clint said. "Doc Thomas will look in on Danny a few times."

"What about our buckboard?"

"I'll have the buckboard and team looked after until you pick it up," Clint said. "I can drive it over to Jamie's, when I pick up my horse."

"Okay, that's good," Kenny said.

"Now why don't you just get some rest yourself," Clint said. "I'll be back in a little while."

"Where are you goin'?" Kenny asked.

"I'm going to see if I can find out anything about who shot Danny," Clint said. "And, when I come back, "I'll bring some food."

"Okay," Kenny said, getting on the bed next to his brother. As Clint left, Kenny was lying on his left side, watching his brother breathe.

Chapter Nineteen

There were still some civilians milling about both inside and out of the hotel, discussing the shooting. Clint walked through the lobby, attracting some of their glances, and stepped outside.

He took a moment to survey the area from the hotel porch, then walked across the street. There were some shops there, which were all open at the moment. He doubted two shooters could have taken up position inside any of them without attracting attention.

That left the rooftops.

There had to be a way to get up there without going inside. He walked around to the back and found it, a stairway to the roof, which must have existed for the purposes of sanitation.

He went up the stairs and walked to the front edge of the roof. There he found some ejected shells from two different rifles, a Remington and a Winchester. He thought about taking them with him, but decided to leave them there in case the constable finally decided to come up to investigate.

He looked down, saw that he had a perfect vantage point of where the buckboard had been sitting. If they had wanted him, it would have been easy to pick him off. That meant Danny was the target, and maybe Kenny, as well.

What could those two kids have done to make some- one want to kill them?

***

When he got back to his room, both boys were asleep. That reminded him that he had to go back down to the lobby and get another room for himself. He was about to leave when Danny opened his eyes.

"Hey, kid," Clint said. "How are you feeling?"

"Stiff," Danny said. "And it hurts."

"Well," Clint said, "you got shot. That always hurts."

"So you been shot a lot?"

"Many times."

"This is my first time," Danny said. "Does it hurt less next time?"

"Danny," Clint said, "let's just hope there isn't a next time."

"Yeah." His eyelids drooped, Clint decided to ask a question before he fell asleep again.

"Danny," Clint said, "who would want to shoot you and Kenny?"

"Nobody wantsta shoot Kenny," Danny said. "It's me."

"Then who was it?"

Sleepily, Danny said, "Coulda only been Eddie Garvin."

"Who's Eddie?"

"He's got a buncha kids stealin' for him," Danny said. "I usedta, but I stopped becuz I don't want Kenny to work for him."

"And he'd shoot you for that?"

"He don't want any of the other kids ta leave 'im." He yawned. "I'm sleepy."

"Okay," Clint said. "Go back to sleep, only . . . where would I find Eddie?"

"There's a big buildin' on DuPont Street," Danny said. "It's his."

"DuPont Street," Clint repeated. "Okay, kid, I'll see you later."

Danny was already asleep.

Clint went down to the lobby and arranged another room for himself.

"Are you, uh, going to pay for that one, sir?" the clerk asked.

"Yes," Clint said, "don't worry. I'm paying."

The clerk gave him a key.

"Anything else, sir?"

"Yeah," Clint said. "how do I get to DuPont Street?"

Chapter Twenty

There was still plenty of the day left for Clint to go to DuPont Street. It was in an older area, with a lot of abandoned buildings, the biggest of which was at the end of the street.

He decided not to go busting in, but to take a look at the activity first. After a couple of hours, he saw that Danny was right. There were kids going in-and-out of the building, usually carrying something when they went in, and empty-handed when they came out.

The situation made Clint think of Fagin, the character from Charles Dickens' novel OLIVER TWIST. Fagin was a pickpocket who taught kids the art, including the Artful Dodger, and Oliver, himself. He wondered if this man Eddie Garvin had ever read the book?

It was still a couple of hours before dark when Clint decided to go in. He waited until a boy of about twelve approached the door, and then fell into step behind him.

"What the—"

"Just keep walking, kid," Clint said. "Take me to Eddie."

"Hey, you ain't the law!" the kid groused.

"That's right, kid," Clint said. "I'm worse."

Clint pushed the boy ahead of him, followed through the gloom to a light up ahead. When they came to the light, Clint saw a man sitting in a chair, with some kids seated on the floor around him.

"What the hell—" the man said. "Who're you?"

"Everybody out!" Clint yelled. When nobody moved, he drew his gun and fired one shot. The kids all jumped to their feet. "Everybody out, and don't ever come back!"

The kids, who looked like they ranged from eight to fourteen, ran for the door.

The man started to stand, but Clint pointed his gun at him.

"Stay where you are!"

The man sank back into his chair. He was in his fifties, with grey hair and a pot belly. Clint waited for the sound of the running kids to fade away.

"Are you Eddie Garvin?" Clint asked.

"That's right," Garvin said. "Who the hell are you? Whataya think yer doin'?"

"I'm here because of Kenny and Danny McBain."

"Oh yeah?" Garvin said. "Is Danny ready to come back to work? And bring Kenny with 'im?"

"Well," Clint said, "Danny survived the two guys you sent to kill him."

"Is that right?" Garvin said. "Somebody tried to kill them? How?"

"You know how," Clint said. "Two shooters, sent to kill a little boy."

"You think you'll survive two shooters?"

Suddenly, two men in the shadows behind him moved, and Clint knew he couldn't hesitate. He fired quickly, four shots, just to be sure. He heard two bodies hit the floor.

"Is that all you have here, Garvin?" Clint asked.

"I'm afraid so."

"Then let's go back to talking about the two little boys, Clint said, while replacing his empty shells with live rounds. Garvin seemed impressed that he could accomplish that so quickly.

"These kids ain't little boys, Mister," Garvin said.

"No, they're not," Clint said. "Not after you've done your Fagin act on them."

"Fagin?" Garvin laughed. "Yeah, Fagin. I like that."

"So you've read Dickens."

"Oh yeah," Garvin said, settling back in his chair comfortably. "I read plenty. Poe, Dickens, Mark Twain."

Apparently, this version of Fagin was an educated man.

"So you modeled yourself after Fagin?"

"Not at all," Garvin said, "but now that you've pointed out the similarity, I can see it."

"Well, the similarity is over," Clint said. "You're over. And you're going to leave the McBain boys alone."

"And if I don't?" Garvin said.

"Then I'll be back to kill you."

"If you don't kill me now, when you come back, you'll never get to me."

"I think I will," Clint said.

"Who are you, anyway?" Garvin asked. "I thought those boys had no relatives. Those are the only ones I take."

"I'm not related to them," Clint said. "I'm their friend. My name's Clint Adams."

"Clint . . . Adams?"

"You've heard of me?"

"I told you," Garvin said, sitting up straight, "I read. And I've read about the Gunsmith. What are you doin' in Florida? Your legend is in the West."

"I'm not here as a legend," Clint said. "I'm here as a man. A man who will kill you if any harm comes to those boys."

"Well," Garvin said, "from what I've read—and what you just did—I know you've killed a lot of people, so I guess you're serious."

"I am."

"Okay then," Garvin said. "Tell Kenny and Danny I'll forget about them."

"I want you to forget about all these kids, Garvin," Clint said.

"Now, that don't make sense."

"Why not?"

"Because if I do that, they'll all starve," Garvin said. "They come here, and I feed them, clothe them, and give them a place to sleep."

"So you're saying they have no one else but you?"

"That's right," Garvin said. "For all intents and purposes, they're my kids. Unless you wanna take responsibility for them all?"

Clint knew he couldn't do that. He was going to have to be happy with convincing Eddie Garvin to leave Kenny and Danny alone.

"You can't change everything overnight, you know," Garvin said.

"Danny's recovering from his gunshot," Clint said. "Leave him and Kenny alone."

"If you leave me alone," Garvin said.

"Deal," Clint said.

"Agreed," Garvin said.

For now, Clint added mentally, and left.

Chapter Twenty-One

When Clint got back to the hotel, it was after dark. He carried the food he had bought from a nearby café and entered the room. The boys were both awake, sitting up on the bed and talking.

"Hey, food!" Kenny said.

"Shrimp?" Danny asked.

"You bet," Clint said.

He sat on the bed with them, looked around for something to put on the bed so that grease didn't get into the sheets. There was nothing, so he grabbed a dirty shirt, spread it out, and put the bag of food on it.

He had brought plenty of napkins, and they ate the shrimp and the potatoes with their fingers, washed it down with the bottle of milk he had also brought.

"Okay, listen up," he said, when they were done, and he had cleaned up. "I have to leave Pensacola tomorrow, but I'll be back."

"When?" Kenny asked.

"I don't know," Clint said, "but I convinced Eddie Garvin to leave you guys alone."

"Really?" Kenny said.

"Yes, really."

"How did you get him to do that?" Danny asked.

"I told him I'd kill him if he bothered you."

"You did?" Kenny asked. "Really?"

"Yes, really."

"So nobody's gonna try ta shoot us anymore?" Kenny asked.

"Nobody is," Clint said. "And when I get back, I'll check in on you guys. Meanwhile you have the finder's fee money I gave you."

"We do?" Danny asked.

"I forgot ta tell ya" Kenny said. "It's under the pillow."

Danny fished it out, counted it and said, "Fifty dollars?"

"Yes," Clint said, "I figured you deserved a little more."

"Wow, Clint, thanks," Danny said.

"Okay," Clint said, standing up, "I got another room, so I'm going to leave and get some sleep. I'll look in on you in the morning before I leave. And then the doctor will be around later." He gathered up all the garbage. "'night, boys."

"G'night, Clint," Kenny said.

As Clint went out the door, the boys were counting the money again.

***

Clint slept well and woke at first light. He had gotten a room down the hall from the boys after checking to see if Lily was still in the hotel. She wasn't. Now he got dressed and packed and went to look in on them. When he opened the door and stuck his head in, they were fast asleep on the bed, so he backed out without waking them up.

He went downstairs, checked out, but made sure the clerk knew the boys were still in his first room.

"Yes, sir, I have my orders they're to be allowed to stay til the end of the week."

"That's good."

"Do you need transportation, sir?"

"No, I'm good," Clint said. "I'll be leaving after breakfast."

"Yes, sir," the clerk said. "Have a good trip."

Clint was eating his ham-and-eggs breakfast when Constable Snyder entered and approached his table. He'd had many breakfasts interrupted like this by lawmen in the past and knew the best way to handle it.

"Have a seat, Constable," he said. "Coffee?"

"Yes, thanks."

Clint poured it for him, then went back to his breakfast.

"Hope you don't mind if I eat while we talk," he said.

"Not at all."

"Did you go up on the rooftop across the street?" Clint asked.

"I did," the constable said, "and I found the spent shells from two different rifles. It's as you said. Two shooters."

Clint nodded.

"So, since you were on the roof ahead of me, what else have you found out?" Snyder asked.

Clint decided to tell him.

Chapter Twenty-Two

"You're sure about Garvin?"

"I am."

"And you think you scared him?"

"I think I convinced him to leave Kenny and Danny alone," Clint answered.

"And the other kids?"

"I couldn't do anything for them," he said. "I don't have the time."

Snyder played with his half empty coffee cup for a moment.

"Well," he said, "I do."

"I was hoping you'd say that."

"The only problem is, I'm the only one here."

"No other constables?"

Snyder shook his head.

"But you killed two of Eddie's men," Snyder said. "It'll take him some time to replace them."

"How long?"

"He won't take just anybody," Snyder said. "When will you be back? I mean, assuming you're coming back."

"I'll be back, but I don't know when."

"Then I might have to act before you return," Snyder said.

"You'd be safer acting before he can replace those men."

"I know," Snyder said. "I only need to know where Garvin is."

"I can tell you where he was," Clint said. "A big building at the end of DuPont Street."

"Ah," Snyder said, "he's used that place before, then abandoned it. I guess he figured he was safe to go back."

Clint looked at the gun the constable wore high on his left hip. It looked like an old Colt.

Snyder saw where he was looking.

"I may not be the gun hand you are," he said, "but I can hit what I shoot at. I'll be fine."

"I'd stay and help if I could," Clint said, "but I have to go."

"I understand," Snyder said. "I figure since you went out to Fort Pickens, you're probably doing something for the government."

Clint didn't answer.

Snyder stood up.

"Whatever you're doing, good luck," the constable said.

"To you, too," Clint said.

Snyder nodded his thanks and left.

Clint paid his bill, grabbed his bag and also left, heading for Jamie's stable.

***

When he got there, Jamie had the horse saddled for him. He told the man what had happened to the boys.

"Are they all right?"

"They are, for now," Clint said. "They're in a room at my hotel. There's a doctor who's going to look after Danny, but he'll be gone the end of the week and they'll have to leave the hotel."

"They're good boys," Jamie said. "I'll make sure they're all right."

"That's what I wanted to hear," Clint said. "Like I told them and Constable Snyder, I'll be back, but I don't know when."

"Well," Jamie said, "you're renting my horse, so I figured you'd be bringin' it back . . . some time."

Clint nodded, walked the horse outside and mounted up. The saddle was worn and old, but the mare was in good condition. Jamie had managed to supply a rifle for him as well, an older model Winchester.

"I'll bring everything back," he promised.

"I figured you would," Jaime said.

***

Clint left Pensacola, headed directly West to Jacksonville. He didn't push the mare at first, preferring instead to get to know her, and let her get to know him. After three days of riding and camping, he figured they had bonded, so that morning he started to push her, and she responded well.

He thought about the two boys along the way, and then gave even more thought to Geronimo and his family. Was this really what the government had asked him to come down here and do? Or did it have more to do with what Jeremy Pike had asked him to do? This meeting with this fella from Cuba?

He camped the fourth night outside of Jacksonville, which appeared to be as large a city as Denver. He decided to skirt the city rather than ride through it, and head southwest to St. Augustine. He had no idea what that town was going to be like. All he knew was that it was one of the oldest in the United States.

When he woke in the morning and mounted the mare, he figured he would make St. Augustine by nightfall.

Chapter Twenty-Three

The first thing he did when he reached St. Augustine was board his horse and check into a hotel. There was an old feel to the town, which made sense since it *was* old. The dirt streets and adobe buildings were things he had seen in Mexico, but the feel was totally different. About the only thing he could equate it to was the French Quarter, in New Orleans. Except for the vegetation, which was palm trees, rather than Southern Magnolias or Cypress. But the streets, some of the buildings and balconies, made him think of the Quarter.

After he got his room, he went out and walked down to the water and got his first look at Fort Marion. It was the oldest masonry fort in the country, with a decided Spanish look to it. It was late in the day, so he decided he'd stop by there the first thing in the morning, after breakfast. He was going to have to talk with Lieutenant Colonel Loomis L. Langdon—but about what?

Walking back to his hotel, he passed a small café where people were sitting outside, looking at the water. It wasn't something he would normally do, sit out in the open, but he had just arrived. He decided to take the chance, just so he could get the feel of the place.

He ordered a cup of coffee and wondered, as he watched some of the boats come in, if he could see Pelican Pete Davis from there.

If he turned his head to the left, he could see the fort. He thought he should probably go there first, before looking for this Pelican Pete.

"Would you like something to eat?" the waiter asked.

"Maybe later," Clint said. "Right now, the coffee's fine."

"As you wish."

"There is something you can help me with, though," Clint said, as the man started away. He was a small man in his fifties. "How long have you lived here?" Clint asked.

"All my life."

"What can you tell me about the fort?"

"The Castillo de San Marcos?"

"No, I mean, Fort Marion."

"Yes, it's the same," the man said. "We who live here call it by its first name, the Castillo de San Marcos. It was Union soldiers who changed the name to Fort Marion."

"And turned it into a prison, right?"

"That's right."

"Is there ever any trouble there?" Clint asked.

"All kinds," the man said. "After all, it's a prison."

"True," Clint said. "Has anything gone on there lately?"

"Just the deaths."

"What?"

"Prisoners are getting sick and dying," the waiter said. "Folks are kinda worried it might be something that might spread, you know?"

"Has the army said anything to assure the locals that won't happen?"

"Naw," the waiter said, "they never even talk to us."

"Are you worried? Being this close to the fort?"

"No, not me."

"Why not?"

"I don't get sick," the waiter said.

"Never?"

"Never."

"That's a good thing," Clint said.

"Yeah, it is," the waiter said. "You sure you don't want something to eat?"

"Not right now," Clint said. "I think I might take a walk down by the water."

"You know," the man said, "the Confederacy tried to take the fort from the water, but they couldn't do it."

"That was a long time ago, though."

"Oh yeah," the waiter said. "I was in my late twenties back then, and I remember the battle real well. The cannons were loud."

"Where'd you hear them from?" Clint asked.

"Right here," the waiter said. "I was working right here."

Someone from another table called him and he said, "I gotta go."

"Sure, thanks."

The waiter walked away, and Clint went back to drinking his coffee and alternating between looking at the fort, and the water.

***

He returned to his hotel and sat outside until he got hungry. The hotel was small and had no dining room, so he walked a couple of blocks until he came to a restaurant and went inside. This time he asked for a back table, and got it, then enjoyed a plate that was a combination of steak and shrimp. He had formed a liking for the shrimp, which was something he wasn't going to be able to get when he went back west.

Idly, he wondered how Kenny and Danny were doing, and hoped he could wrap things up here quickly and get back to Pensacola to check on them.

Chapter Twenty-Four

In the morning Clint went back to the café by the water where he'd been watching the boats. The same waiter came over to take his order.

"Somethin' to eat this time?"

"Some bacon-and-eggs would be good."

"And then?"

"What do you mean?"

"I mean will you be going down by the water after, or to the fort?"

"What makes you think either?"

"You sat here last night trying to make up your mind, right?"

"Well," Clint said, "maybe I haven't quite made up my mind, yet."

"I'll get you your breakfast, and some coffee."

"You do that."

Clint watched the boats go out—the night before he had been watching them come in—while he waited for his food. This was going to be the last time he sat out in the open in St. Augustine. After today, some folks were going to know who he was.

The waiter brought the pot of coffee and plate of bacon-and-eggs at the same time, set them down.

"I've got a question for you," Clint said. "Since you've lived here so long and have spent so much time right here."

The waiter folded his arms.

"Go ahead," he said.

"First," Clint said, as he bit into a piece of bacon, "what's your name?"

"Arlo Crowder."

"You got family down here, Arlo?"

"I do."

"Do you know a man named Pelican Peter Davis?"

"Sure I do," Arlo said. "Everybody around here knows Pelican Pete."

"As what?"

"As what he is," Arlo said. "A smuggler. Is that who you've got business with?"

"Thanks for the breakfast, Arlo."

Arlo smiled.

"Pete's boat is one of those that just went out," he said. "You'll have to wait for him to come back to see him. You let me know if you need anything else."

"You'll be the first. Thanks, Arlo."

***

Clint presented himself at the front gate of Fort Marion and asked to see Lieutenant Colonel Loomis Langdon.

"And what's your name?" the Union soldier on guard asked. He had a Corporal's stripes on his arms.

"Clint Adams."

The man's eyebrows went up.

"That for real?" he asked.

"It's for real."

"Well, damn," the soldier said. "What's the Gunsmith doing in Florida?"

"So far," Clint said, "just eating shrimp."

"Stay right there," the guard said. "I'll be right back."

The guard went inside the fort through a smaller door next to the large gate.

Staring up at the walls of Fort Marion—or The Castillo, as the locals called it—Clint wondered if this mass of masonry was the closest thing America had to a castle?

When the door opened again, the Corporal stepped out, but didn't close it behind him. Another soldier came out and assumed the position as guard in front of the door.

"Come on, Mr. Gunsmith," the Corporal said, "The Lieutenant Colonel says he'll see you."

"Thank you, Corporal."

He followed the Corporal back through the door, and then across a wide expanse of yard before they came to a building.

"So you never had shrimp before you came down here?" the soldier asked.

"Nope."

"And you like it?"

"Not as much as I like steak," Clint said, "but yes."

"Then you ain't had really good shrimp yet," the Corporal said.

"No?" Clint said. "Maybe before I leave, you can tell me where to go to get it?"

"I sure will," the Corporal said. "I'll tell ya as I walk ya back out."

"I appreciate it."

"You here to see a prisoner?" the soldier asked.

"No," Clint said, "just to talk to the Colonel."

"Well, take my advice," the Corporal said, "treat the Colonel like he's a General."

"Why's that?"

"Because that's how he acts."

Chapter Twenty-Five

The Corporal knocked on the door that was marked LT. COLONEL LOOMIS L. LANGDON. In prisons most of these types of doors were marked WARDEN. This one said a lot about the man behind it.

"Colonel, this is Clint Adams," the Corporal said, as he opened the door. "Mr. Adams, Lieutenant Colonel Loomis L. Langdon."

"That'll be all, Corporal," the man behind the desk said. "Wait outside."

"Yessir."

The Corporal sent Clint a reminder with his eyes and stepped outside.

"Have a seat, sir," the Colonel said. Clint decided to think of the man only as "The Colonel."

He sat down.

"What can I do for you, Mr. Adams?"

"Have you heard from Washington?" Clint asked.

"Have I heard what from Washington?" the Colonel asked. "They usually let me run this place as I see fit."

"I mean," Clint said, "were you advised I'd be here?"

"No," the Colonel said, "I haven't heard a word from them."

Clint studied the man. He was tall, grey-haired, in his sixties, with a stiff back and chin. He'd known men like this before, unbending, unyielding and, when they were given authority, unbearable.

"Well then," Clint said, "I have to tell you I'm here on behalf of Geronimo."

"What the hell—" the Colonel started, then stopped. "Why would you be here on behalf of that savage?"

"He's not a savage—"

"Oh, don't tell me the Gunsmith is a bleeding heart Indian lover?" the Colonel said.

Clint stared at the man. He had to take a moment so he wouldn't drag the soldier over his desk.

"Geronimo's family is here," Clint said. "And I heard you're having a problem with disease, and death."

"I've got red-skinned savages dropping dead of some disease," the Colonel said. "How is that a problem?"

"What the hell is wrong with you?" Clint asked. "You hate Indians that bad?"

"Yes, I do," the Colonel said. "You got a problem with that?"

Clint stood up and leaned on the Colonel's desk.

"Washington sent me here to tell you to get Geronimo's family out of here," Clint said.

"And send them where?" the Colonel asked.

"To Fort Pickens."

"There are no women or children in Fort Pickens," the Colonel said. "If you were there, you'd know that."

"Then send them somewhere else," Clint said. "Just get them out of here."

"Corporal!"

The door opened and the Corporal came in.

"Sir?"

"Mr. Adams is leaving."

"I'm not done here," Clint said.

"Get four more men if you have to, and carry him out," the Colonel said. "And once he's gone, do not let him back in here."

"Look, you sonofabitch—"

"See here, Adams," the Colonel said, finally standing and getting a little color in his face, "I don't believe Washington sent you here to tell me what to do. I take my orders from them."

"Mr. Adams?" the Corporal said, pointing his rifle at Clint. "Do I need four more men?"

"Maybe not," Clint said, "but you need another commanding officer."

He stormed out, with the Corporal right behind him.

Chapter Twenty-Six

As the Corporal ushered Clint out the front gate, Clint asked, "Where's the nearest saloon?"

"Right around the corner, sir," the Corporal said. "A lot of us go there."

"The Colonel?"

"Never!"

"Good."

Clint left and headed for the saloon.

***

He got a beer from the bar and took it to a table in the back. As he looked around, he didn't see any soldiers there. He thought they would probably come in when a shift at the prison was over.

He was now convinced that sending him down there to talk to Geronimo was not the real reason Washington had. Perhaps Geronimo had asked for him, but Washington wanted him to come down here for another reason, which probably had to do with Pelican Pete.

He called the bartender over.

"Another one?" the man asked.

"Maybe later," Clint said. "Can you tell me when the boats start coming back in?"

"Usually between three o'clock and when it gets dark."

Judging by the clock on the wall, he had plenty of time.

"Thanks."

He left the saloon and headed for the café where Arlo Crowder worked.

***

"Sure, I can point out his boat to you from here," Arlo said. "They won't start coming in til about three, though."

"I'll be back," Clint said. "Thanks."

He left the café and walked down to the docks, just to have a look. There were one or two boats moored there, with nobody on board, as well as a few men on the dock. Nobody paid any attention to him, despite the fact he was wearing his gun. He didn't know what the law was in Florida about guns and holsters, but so far nobody had said a word to him.

There was room on those docks for twenty, maybe even thirty boats. He was truly going to have to rely on Arlo Crowder to point Pelican Pete out, otherwise he'd have to go from boat to boat.

His meeting with Colonel Langdon was sticking in his craw, as was the thought that he had been manipulated into coming down there by Washington. He only hoped they had also lied to Jim West to get his cooperation.

Rather than stay in a saloon and drink til then, Clint decided to go back to his hotel, then walk back to Arlo's café at three. For the first time he paid attention to the name of the place. It was called Palmetto's.

***

"What the hell is a palmetto?" he asked Arlo when the man came to his table.

"It's a tree," Arlo said. "What can I get you?"

"A cup of coffee and a piece of pie. What kind do you have?"

"Key Lime."

"Anything else?"

"Just key lime," Arlo said. "It's what everybody down here eats."

"Okay, bring me a slice of key lime pie," Clint said. "And tell me when you see Pelican Pete's boat."

"Gotcha."

Arlo brought the pie and coffee, then went to wait on some other customers. Clint choked on the first bite of key lime pie, then had a second, then a third.

"How'd you like it?" Arlo asked.

"Tart, but not bad," Clint said. "Have you seen Pete's boat yet?"

"Not yet."

"Then I'll have another slice, and more coffee."

"Comin' up."

***

After three slices of key lime, Clint found he had to stop. He was having a beer instead of more coffee when Arlo came over to the table.

"There it is," Arlo pointed, "the blue one with the striped sail."

Clint looked, saw the boat Arlo was talking about.

"How far out is he?" he asked.

"He should be docking in about seven minutes."

"You know it that close?" Clint asked.

"Oh yeah," Arlo said. "Point to any boat and I'll tell you when it's docking."

Clint stood up, dropped some money on the table.

"That's too much for the pie," Arlo said.

"It's not just for the pie," Clint said, "Thanks."

***

By the time he got down to the docks, a crowd seemed to have gathered at the end of the pier. There were two boats moored there, one on each side, and one was blue with a striped sail.

He made his way down to the end of the pier, where a group of men were standing over something.

He was about to join them when two men in uniform came down the pier and moved past him. They were lawmen, wearing uniforms, indicating that St. Augustine had itself a more modern police department than Pensacola.

Clint stood back while the two men tried to disperse the crowd. As the spectators headed back up the pier and past Clint he asked, "What's going on?"

"Somebody killed one of the fishermen as he was gettin' off his boat," a man told him.

"Is that right?" Clint asked. "How'd it happen?"

"Looks like somebody knifed 'im."

"Did you know him?"

"Yeah, hell, everybody knew him," the man said. "His name was Pelican Pete."

Chapter Twenty-Seven

Clint went back to the Palmetto.

"What happened?" Arlo asked. "I saw a crowd down there."

"Somebody killed Pelican Pete," Clint said, sitting at a table inside the place.

"What? Why?"

"That's what I was going to ask you," Clint said. "Why would somebody kill him?"

"Well," Arlo said, sitting across from him, "He's a smuggler. So somebody who was doin' business with him might kill him."

"That's what I thought," Clint said. "Who's the law here?"

"What about it?"

"I saw two men in uniform," Clint said.

"Oh, that, yeah," Arlo said, "we have a sheriff, but now there's a police department, too."

"And this sheriff," Clint said, "is he an old timer, or a younger man?"

"Oh, he's old school," Arlo said. "In fact, his father used to be sheriff here, and now he's been the sheriff for over twenty years."

"What's his name?"

"Sheriff Roy Jensen. His office is around the corner from here. In fact, I'm surprised he wasn't down at the pier. Jesus, Pete's dead?"

"Yeah. What about the soldiers from the fort?"

"What about them?"

"Do they get involved in law enforcement at all?" Clint asked. "I mean, it's not a big town—"

"Naw," Arlo said, "they pretty much just keep to prison business."

"Speaking of that," Clint said, "how do the locals feel about the people in the prison who are dying?"

"It's prisoners dying," Arlo said. "Nobody's cares about that."

"Are you sure?"

"Oh, yeah," Arlo said. "None of our citizens have died as a result."

"One last thing," Clint said.

"Go ahead."

"What's good here for supper?"

Arlo stood up.

"I'll surprise you."

***

When Clint finished eating, he washed it down with another beer.

"How was it?" Arlo asked.

"It was good," Clint said. "Kind of spicy. It tasted a lot like chicken. Was it chicken?"

"Yeah, that's what everybody thinks," Arlo said. "It was 'gator."

"What?"

"Alligator."

Clint stared at him a moment.

"Are you kidding?"

"No."

"I didn't know you could cook and eat alligator."

"Well, you can," Arlo said. "People down here like it a lot."

"Well, I can see why, I guess," Clint said. "It was . . . tasty."

"Glad to hear it," Arlo said. "So, what are you gonna do about Pelican Pete?"

"What makes you think I'm going to do anything about him?" Clint asked.

Arlo looked around. The place was starting to get busy for supper.

"You had business with him," Arlo said. "Now what are you gonna do?"

"I don't know," Clint said.

"You gotta find out who killed 'im."

"Why do I have to find out who killed him?" Clint asked. "You've got police, and a sheriff."

"Yeah, well you're government, ain'tcha?" Arlo asked, keeping his voice down. "A marshal, or something?"

"What makes you say that?"

"You ask a lot of questions, you went to the prison, and you were askin' about Pete," Arlo said, ticking the points off on his fingers. "Who the hell else would be asking about a smuggler?"

"I'm not a marshal," Clint said.

Arlo looked around, then leaned closer.

"But you are government, right?"

Clint hesitated, then said, "Not exactly."

"Well," Arlo said, "I've got other tables. If you still want my help, let me know."

"I will."

Clint paid his bill and left Palmetto. He headed around the corner, where Arlo said the sheriff's office was.

Chapter Twenty-Eight

Clint found the sheriff's office, a small, shabby wood building that looked like a larger version of an outhouse. He knocked on the door and entered, found a man in his late forties sitting at a small desk. With the two of them inside, the office felt crowded. There were obviously no jail cells.

"Jesus," Clint said, "where do you put your prisoners?"

"Like they let me arrest anybody," the man said. "Can I help you?"

"Are you Sheriff Roy Jensen?"

"That's me," Jensen said. "Who sent you over here?"

"Nobody sent me, but it was Arlo over at the Palmetto who told me where to find you."

"Arlo's good people," Jensen said. "You a friend of his?"

"Yes, I am."

"Let's get out of here, then," Jensen said, standing. "This place ain't big enough for both of us."

As they both stepped outside, Clint asked, "Why don't they give you a bigger office?"

"Because they want me to quit," Jensen said. "But I ain't gonna give 'em the satisfaction. So, who are you and whataya want?"

"My name's Clint Adams."

"Yeah," Jensen said, "and I'm Wyatt Earp. What the hell would the Gunsmith be doin' in St. Augustine?"

"Well, I *was* looking for Pelican Pete."

"Oh, you're outta luck," Jensen said. "They found him dead this afternoon."

"I know, I was down there," Clint said. "I was waiting to meet him, and somebody killed him before I could get to him."

"Wait a minute," Jensen said. "Are you really Clint Adams?"

"I'm really Clint Adams."

"And you came here to meet with Pete?"

"To talk to him," Clint said. "We never met, before."

"What would the Gunsmith want with a smuggler?"

"Just to talk."

"About what?"

"Look," Clint said, "I just need to know who'd want to kill him."

"Anybody he did business with."

"Will you be looking into it?" Clint asked.

"Me? Hell, no, that's somethin' the damn new police department'll be workin' on. Go talk to them."

"I just thought you'd know more about what's going on than they would. According to Arlo, you've been around here a long time."

"Look," Jensen said, "I can tell you Pelican Pete had more enemies than friends. How was he killed?"

"He was stabbed."

"Oh."

"Why?"

"There's a man who's lived here a long time," Jensen said. "Like Pete, he don't have a lot of friends, and he's been known to kill an enemy or two."

"So?"

"With a knife," Jensen said.

"Ah."

"But if you go to see him, you gotta be careful," Jensen said. "He wrestles alligators, and he not only likes knives, but he's used a machete."

"And this new police department, they know about him?"

"Everybody knows about him," Jensen said. "His name's Bradford O'Neil, but folks around here call him Gator, for obvious reasons."

"Because he wrestles them?"

"Because he looks like one."

"How does somebody look like an alligator?" Clint asked.

"You'll see, my friend," Jensen said, "you'll see."

***

Following Sheriff Jensen's directions, Clint found the police department building. It was obviously the newest structure in St. Augustine, pristine white.

They had a fresh-faced young man in uniform stationed at a front desk. He smiled at Clint as he entered.

"Can I help you, sir?"

"Yes," Clint said, "I'd like to see someone about Pelican Pete."

"Pelican Pete . . . Davis?"

"Yeah," Clint said, "the fisherman who was killed down on the docks this afternoon."

"What do you know about it?"

"Nothing," Clint said. "That's why I'm here."

"Well, then," the man said, "you'd have to talk to Lieutenant Flynn about that."

"Is the Lieutenant here?" Clint asked.

"What's your name, sir?"

"Clint Adams."

"Let me check and see," the young officer said. "He might still be out on Pete's murder."

"Good," Clint said, "I'll wait."

Chapter Twenty-Nine

Lieutenant Flynn was another young man—not as young as the one on the desk—and not as fresh-faced—but younger than Clint expected. If he was thirty, Clint would have been surprised.

"Officer Peabody says you might know something about Pete Davis' murder," Flynn said, when he appeared from somewhere inside the building.

"That's not exactly right," Clint said. "I was supposed to meet with Pete Davis, but somebody killed him first. I wanted to find out what you knew about it."

Flynn was in shirtsleeves, having left his jacket on his chair.

"Let's take a walk," he said.

They stepped outside and started walking.

"Okay," Flynn said, "I didn't want anybody inside to hear this, but Peabody told me your name is Clint Adams."

"That's right."

"So you're the Gunsmith, right?"

"That's right."

"What did you want with Davis?"

"Well," Clint said, "to tell you the truth, I don't even know. A friend of mine asked me to stop and see him."

"And didn't tell you about what?"

"No." It was the truth, as far as it went.

"So you don't have any idea who killed him," Flynn said.

"No," Clint said, "I only got here yesterday. I don't know anybody except the waiter at the Palmetto."

"Palmetto?" Flynn said. "I haven't eaten there."

"How long have you lived here?" Clint asked.

"I only got this job two months ago," Flynn said. "I don't know anybody in town, either."

Clint stopped walking.

"So you don't know anything about Pelican Pete?" he asked.

"Only that he was supposed to be a smuggler," Flynn said. "Look, you've had experience, maybe you can help me out."

"That's why you didn't want to talk in the building?" Clint asked. "Because you were going to ask me for help?"

"I'm pretty new at this—"

"What'd you do before you got this job?"

"I was a, uh, teacher up in Philadelphia. I came down here for a change,"

"Jesus," Clint said. Between Sheriff Jensen and Flynn, neither of them was going to figure out who killed Pelican

Pete. So, the only way Clint would find out what Pete was going to give him was to figure it out for himself.

"Thanks a lot, Lieutenant."

"For what?' Flynn asked.

"For nothing," Clint said, and walked away.

***

Clint decided since the only person he really knew in St. Augustine was Arlo, he'd go back to Palmetto and talk to him again.

"Flynn, you said?" Arlo asked. "I don't know him."

"Arlo," Clint said, sitting at a table inside the now deserted café, "now I know the sheriff and the police aren't going to be able to find out who killed Pelican Pete."

"So you're gonna do it?" Arlo asked.

"We're going to do it," Clint said.

"Why me?" Arlo asked.

"Because you're the only person I know in St. Augustine."

"What about the soldiers at the fort?"

"I wouldn't depend on them any more than I would the sheriff or the police. Especially not that Lieutenant Flynn."

"Well," Arlo said, "*I'm* probably the only person who actually liked Pete, so consider me on board. What do we do first?"

"I'd like to get a look at his boat," Clint said.

"I close in an hour," Arlo said. "You want to do it to-night?"

"I was thinking about tomorrow morning, but why not?" Clint asked.

"Good," Arlo said, "you can stay here and wait, or come back in an hour."

"I've got nothing else to do," Clint said, "so I'll wait."

"Then let me start cleaning up," Arlo said.

***

While Clint sat there, drinking coffee and waiting, he realized if he hadn't come all the way down to Florida—if he was in some place like Texas or New Mexico—he'd just ride out and forget about it. After all, he had been lied to by General Hammond and probably by Jeremy Pike. The only thing that confused him was Geronimo. It was doubtful that the government had gotten the Apache medicine man to lie to him, as well. He felt bad that it looked like he wasn't able to do anything for the old Indian's family.

"All set," Arlo said. "I'll lock up and we'll walk down to the dock."

"Will anybody stop us?" Clint asked, as Arlo locked the door.

"I don't know," Arlo said. "I ain't never done this before."

"Okay, well," Clint said, "let's go and find out."

Chapter Thirty

They walked down to the pier, which was dark and deserted.

"No lights?" Clint asked.

"Not yet," Arlo said, "not down here."

There was enough moonlight for them to walk to the end of the pier without falling off, but it was going to be dark on the boat.

"Maybe we better come back in the morning," Clint said.

"I'm sure there's gonna be a lamp on the boat," Arlo said.

"Okay. Let's look."

When they reached the boat, Clint saw that the sail had been taken down. They stepped aboard, and he found it more spacious than he had thought.

"It's a fishing boat," Arlo said, "and he must've used it for his, uh, smuggling."

"Right, right."

"Here's a lamp." Arlo struck a match, lit the lamp, and they started looking around the boat.

"What are we lookin' for?" Arlo asked.

"To be honest, I don't know," Clint said.

They found a compartment where Pete probably hid some of the contraband he smuggled, but it was empty.

"Nothing," Arlo said.

"Yeah, I can see that," Clint said. "I think we're done here."

They got off the boat, stood on the pier and looked out at the water, with the moonlight reflecting off it.

"You're not used to this, are you?" Arlo asked.

"No," Clint said, "out west we watch the moonlight on the desert, or the mountains, sometimes shining off a lake, but nothing like this." He looked at the boat again. "What's going to happen to the boat?"

"As far as I know, the only family Pelican Pete had was his wife."

"What? He was married?"

"That's what I heard."

"Well," Clint said, "then I've got to talk to her. Do you know where she lives?"

"I know where Pete lived, but I'm not sure if she lives there. I don't even know if they were still together."

"Could you find out, Arlo?"

"Yeah," he said, "yeah, I'll ask around."

"Good," Clint said. "I'll check back with you tomorrow and see if you found out anything."

"Sure," Arlo said, "come by at lunch time."

"Not breakfast?"

"You can come for breakfast, but I open early, and I won't be able to look for Pete's wife until after."

"Okay," Clint said, "make it lunch."

They walked back up from the docks to the street, and there they split up, with Clint walking back to his hotel.

***

In the morning he had breakfast in his hotel dining room, eating it slowly while he considered his situation. If Arlo found Pelican Pete's wife, he'd have somebody to talk to, maybe a direction to go. If not, then what was he doing down there? With Pete dead, it might be all over. There was no way to find out what Pelican Pete had for him, and no way to help Geronimo's family. The only thing left for him to do might be going back to the West, where he belonged.

But first, he had to find out if Arlo had found the wife.

"Anything else, sir?" the skinny waiter asked.

"Just some more coffee," Clint said, "then I'll get out of here."

"You're a guest of the hotel, sir," the waiter said, "you can sit here as long as you like."

"Thanks."

***

Rather than sit in the hotel dining room until lunch time, Clint decided to go back to his room. He was still trying to convince himself it was worth sticking it out in Florida a little longer, since he had also promised Kenny and Danny that he would be back in Pensacola.

It was almost noon when he finally left the room and walked down to Palmetto. There were already a good number of customers at some of the tables, but Arlo had made sure Clint had one in the back.

"Anything?" he asked.

"I still got a couple of tables to handle," Arlo said. "Lemme take care of them, and bring you something for lunch, and then we'll talk."

"Okay, then," Clint agreed, "go ahead and surprise me, but nothing big."

"Okay."

As Arlo went to the kitchen, Clint sat back in his chair, watched the other diners, wondering if any of them were having alligator.

Chapter Thirty-One

"I found her," Arlo said, sitting across from Clint.

"Where?" Clint asked. "I hope it's someplace around here."

"Definitely," Arlo said. "She wasn't living with him, but she's in St. Augustine."

Clint took a spoonful of something Arlo told him was turtle soup. At first, he didn't believe him, but it seemed to taste okay.

"Will I need my horse, or can I walk there from here?" Clint asked.

"No, we can walk."

"We?"

"Well, I'll have to introduce you," Arlo said. "Turns out, I know 'er. She's eaten here."

"That'll come in handy, then," Clint said. "Yeah, good, an introduction will work."

"I'm gonna close after lunch, take you over there, and then come back for supper."

"Fine."

"Finish your soup and I'll get rid of these last few customers."

"Go ahead."

By the time he emptied his bowl, Arlo came over and collected it. All the other diners had gone, so he took the empty bowl to the kitchen, then came back and locked the door as they left.

The house was six blocks away, but was positioned so that Clint could still see the fort when they got there.

"This is it?" he asked.

"Yep."

It was a very small, wood-frame house, old but with a new coat of paint on it. They approached the front door and Arlo knocked. When the door opened Clint was surprised to find himself looking at a beautiful redhead in her thirties, who frowned at them, until she recognized Arlo.

"You're Arlo, from Palmetto, right?" she asked.

"That's right," Arlo said, "and this is my friend, Clint Adams."

"Hello," she said. "I'm Maggie Davis."

"Mrs. Davis—" Clint started, but she cut him off.

"Please don't call me that," she said. "Pete and I weren't living together anymore. We were getting divorced and I was going back to my maiden name, which was Beechcroft."

"So, Miss Beechcroft, then?"

"Oh hell," she said, "just call me Maggie. Would you both like to come in?"

"I have to get back to Palmetto," Arlo said, "but Clint wanted to talk to you about Pete."

"Ah," she said, "well, all right. I suppose you better come in, then."

She backed away from the doorway and Clint said to Arlo, "Thanks," and followed her inside.

"Can I offer you something to drink?" she asked. Her furniture was mismatched, and looked handmade, but the place was very clean.

She was tall, solidly built, her red hair hanging down past her shoulders, completely straight. The dress she was wearing was thin, and hugged her, outlining her large breasts and nipples very clearly. She noticed the way he was looking at her.

"I'm sorry about what I'm wearing," she said. "I wasn't expecting company."

"That's okay."

"If it bothers you, I can change," she said. "It would only take a minute."

"No, Maggie, it's okay," Clint said.

"Good," she said. "Lemonade?"

"That sounds good." The heat, since he'd gotten to Florida, hadn't been bothering him, but cold lemonade did sound refreshing.

She came back from the kitchen with two tall glasses of lemonade, sweating from the ice inside.

"There you go," she said. "Have a seat, please, Mr. Adams and tell me what I can do for you."

"First I'd like to offer my condolences—"

"Don't bother," she said, cutting him off. "Pete was no great loss, believe me. We've been apart for many months."

"I don't know if you can help me, then," Clint said. "I was supposed to meet with him, and he was going to pass me something."

"And you want to know if I know what it was?"

"Exactly."

She put her glass down and leaned forward on her sofa. He was seated across from her, on the mismatched armchair.

"I don't have any idea," she said. "But what could it have been? Nothing valuable, surely. Do you see this furniture? This is all I could afford with the money he gave me. Are you also going to ask me if I have any idea who killed him?"

"I *was*," he said.

"Put me at the top of the list. I could've killed 'im, myself."

"Well," Clint said, "other than yourself, can you think of anyone else?"

She looked at her lemonade and said, "Maybe if I had a real drink."

Chapter Thirty-Two

Maggie went to the kitchen and came back with a bottle of whiskey. She poured some into her lemonade and held the bottle out to Clint.

"Sure," he said, holding his glass out.

When they both had whiskey in their glasses she sat back down.

"Okay," she said, "he was stabbed, right?"

"Right."

"With a knife or a machete?"

"I don't know."

"It really doesn't matter," she said. "If he was stabbed, then it was probably Gator."

"Bradford O'Neil, right?"

"Who told you? Oh, Arlo."

"Yes."

"Well, I'd put him at number two, after me."

"Not ahead of you?"

She sipped her drink, thought a moment, then said, "Yeah, okay, him number one, me number two."

"And what about number three?"

"Any of the other smugglers around here," she said, "or any of the people doing business with Pete."

"But you don't know who they were?"

"No."

"Maggie, has the law been here to talk to you, yet?"

"You mean like the sheriff?" she asked. "What a waste he is."

"What about a Lieutenant Flynn?"

"Flynn? No, nobody by that name."

"No police from the new department?"

"You mean with that tan uniform?" she asked. "No, no one."

That was about what Clint figured. Nobody was trying to solve the murder of Pelican Pete.

"So it seems like the law doesn't care, right?" she asked.

"That's the way it seems."

"Well," she said, "I'm with them."

"Maggie—"

"Come on, Clint—can I call you Clint?"

"Sure."

"You don't really care who killed him, either," she said. "You just want to know what it was he was going to give you."

"Well, yes, that's true," he said, "but I think part of that is going to be finding out who killed him."

"So you and Arlo are going to do it?"

Clint shrugged.

"Arlo's the only other person I know here in St. Augustine," he explained.

"Well," she said, "now you know me."

"Maggie—"

"And I know who you are, Mr. Gunsmith," she said. "I read those dime novels."

Those damn dime novels, again.

"Don't believe everything you read."

"But you are the Gunsmith, right?"

"That's right."

"Well, that's good," she said, putting her drink down. "Come with me."

"Where are we going?" he asked, setting his glass aside and standing up.

"You'll see," she said, putting her hand out to grab his. "Just come."

She pulled him along from the sitting room into the next room, which he realized was her bedroom.

"Maggie—"

"I told you Pete and I have been apart for a while," she said, turning to face him.

"Yes, you did."

"Which means I haven't had sex in all that time," she went on.

"Maggie—"

"Not that Pete and me, we never had sex all that much," she said. "But I've got to tell you, I was almost ready to settle for little old Arlo when the two of you showed up at my door—thank God."

She reached behind her, which thrust her big breasts forward at him as she undid her dress in the back. When she peeled it off, he saw that, as he had suspected, she was totally naked underneath.

The dress went off to one side and she stood in front of him with her hands on her hips. Her breasts had heavy undersides, with large, rust colored nipples surrounded by freckles.

The hair on her head was dark red, but the bush between her thighs was lighter, more fiery colored. She had wide-hips, rounded thighs and he didn't need to see her from behind to know that he was already in trouble. He would never be able to resist this naked goddess.

"Well?" she asked. "Are you ready?"

"I will be," he said, unstrapping his gun.

Chapter Thirty-Three

By the time he got himself undressed his cock was fully hard and loaded for bear.

"Now you're going to have to show me you're actually the Gunsmith," she challenged.

"I'll do my best, Ma'am," he said.

They came together in a feverish kiss that went on for a long time as their mouths became acquainted. They rubbed their bodies together, and then their hands began to roam. Clint enjoyed letting go for the moment of Geronimo and his family, of Pelican Pete and the government lying to him to get him down here.

He turned her so her back was to the bed and then lowered her onto it. Once he was on top, he went to work with his hands, his mouth, his tongue. He spent a lot of time on her breasts and nipples because, if nothing else, he was a definite breast man and she had the loveliest pair he had seen in a long time. He thought it might've been the freckles that made them even more special.

When he was finally able to pull his attention away from her chest, he worked his way down to her crotch, where she had grown very wet.

"Oh God," she moaned as his tongue probed, "I needed this so bad—and I needed it from a real man!"

From her words he felt they were evenly matched, because he knew, as he slid his hands beneath her to cup her ass, this was a real woman he had in his hands.

As he pressed his face to her, she also started grinding herself against him, gasping, "Oh yeah, oh yeah, oh yeah . . ." over and over. Finally she screamed, reached for his head and held him against her pussy as she gushed all over his face.

He pulled back, mounted her and drove his hard cock into her, causing her eyes to widen and her whole body to tense. As he started fucking her, she wrapped those powerful legs around his waist and held on tight until, finally, he exploded inside of her and she screamed . . .

***

"I'm sorry," she said, later.

"About what?"

"Screaming," she said. "I probably made you deaf, but Jesus, that was . . . it was so good . . ."

"You don't have to apologize to me for what we just did," Clint said. "I think I needed it almost as much as you did."

They were sitting up on the bed, both still naked, and he couldn't take his eyes off her breasts. She looked into his lap, saw him getting hard again.

"Oh my God," she said, "you're not done."

"No," he said, "I'm not, and it's your fault."

"Well then," she said, "if it's my fault, I should do something about it."

She pushed him back down on the bed, then got down between his legs, stroked his cock until it was nice and hard. When it was, she took it in her mouth and sucked him avidly until she finished him.

She sat back on her heels then and, wiping the corners of her mouth with her fingertips, asked, "Is that better?"

"Well . . ."

She looked down between his legs.

"Damn!" she said, then immediately turned and got on her hands and knees, hiking her butt up into the air for him and shaking it . . .

***

She rolled over and looked down at his almost limp cock with a smile.

"Finally?"

"I think so," he said, looking at her breasts, again. "Although . . ."

She pulled the sheet up in front of her.

"Why don't I make us something to eat?" she suggested. "And we can continue our talk."

"Have you thought of someone else who might've killed Pete?"

"No," she said, "but I think I can tell you where to find Gator, if you want to talk to him."

"That sounds like a good idea."

She stood up from the bed, taking the sheet, wrapped it around her.

"What're you doing?" he asked.

"Keeping you from seeing my ass as I leave the room," she said. "You are the Gunsmith, aren't you?"

"Yes, I am."

"You get dressed and come into the kitchen," she said. "I'll have something ready."

"I'll be there."

She reached down, picked up her dress and carried it from the room with her. Next thing he saw was the sheet as it came flying through the doorway, back into the room.

Chapter Thirty-Four

Clint sat at Maggie's kitchen table and she set a plate in front of him.

"Alligator?" he asked.

"You've had it before?"

"Once."

"Well, mine's different," she said. "Have a taste."

He picked up his fork and took a bite.

"Wow, that's good."

"Doesn't taste like chicken, does it?" she asked.

"No," he said, "it doesn't."

"See, people are always saying it tastes like chicken," she said. "I wanted to change that."

He took another bite.

"I think you did it," he said.

She sat across from him with a plate of her own.

"Well, you lived up to part of your reputation," she told him. "And I appreciate it."

"Shucks, Ma'am," he said. "It was my pleasure . . . believe me."

She went to the stove, came back with two cups of coffee.

"So okay," he said, "Gator O'Neil."

"He lives over in Twelve Mile Swamp, near Turnbull Creek."

"A swamp?"

"Oh yeah," she said.

"So that means . . . alligator?" He pointed to his plate.

"He probably wrestled and caught the one you're eating right now," she said, with a smile.

"Does he know you?"

"He does."

"Does he know Arlo?"

"Probably," she said. "I'm sure Arlo buys his gator from Gator."

"Okay then," Clint said, "I'll have Arlo take me to him."

"No," she said, "I better take you."

"Why?"

"He might shoot you, or even Arlo, on sight if you go near his place," she said. "He won't shoot me."

"Why not?"

She smiled.

"Why do you think?"

"You and Gator have a relationship?" Clint asked.

"No," she said, "but he wants one."

"Okay then," Clint said. "When?"

"How about tomorrow morning?" she asked.

"That's fine with me," Clint said.

"Meanwhile," she asked, "what have you got planned for tonight?"

He was tempted to say nothing, but instead he said, "I've got a few stops to make." He didn't think spending the night with her would be a good idea. By morning he'd have nothing left.

"I better get to it," he said. "How about I come by in the morning to get you?"

"You got a horse?" she asked.

"Yes."

"Bring it."

"I will," he said. "Thanks for the gator . . . and everything else."

"Thank you, *Mr.* Gunsmith."

He left Maggie's house on shaky legs.

***

He went back to the docks to take a look around in the daylight. While he was searching the boat again, two men came walking over. They looked like fishermen.

"What are you doin' here?" one of them asked.

"Just looking," Clint said.

Both men stood over six feet with broad shoulders and big hands.

"Get off that boat," the other growled. "It belonged to our friend."

Clint stared up at them.

"The way I heard it," Clint said, "Pelican Pete didn't have any friends."

"Well, friend or not," the first one said, "he was one of us, and you don't belong on his boat."

Clint hadn't found anything, so he voluntarily got off the boat.

"Happy?" he asked.

"No," the first fisherman said. "How do we know you ain't the one who killed 'im?"

"You don't," Clint said, "except I'm telling you I didn't. In fact, I was supposed to meet up with him. He was going to give me something."

"Oh yeah?" the second fisherman asked. "What?"

"I don't know."

"And that's what you was lookin' for on the boat?" the other man asked. "Somethin' you don't know?"

"How do we know you ain't stole somethin' before we stopped ya?" the first man asked. "Empty your pockets."

"I don't think so," Clint said.

"Empty 'em," the second man said, "or we'll empty 'em for ya."

"And we ain't afraid of your gun," the other said. "You ain't gonna shoot two unarmed men."

"I'm not about to take a beating from two overgrown idiots, either," Clint said. "So where do we go from here?"

"We break your neck," the two men said, starting toward him.

"I think they might have another idea," Clint said, pointing.

The two fisherman turned and saw three uniformed policeman coming toward them. Clint recognized one of them as Lieutenant Flynn.

"Is there a problem here?" he asked.

"No problem," Clint said, stepping off the boat. "I was just leaving. These fellas were just helping me out with some information about boats."

"Yeah," one of the fishermen said. "We was helpin' him."

"Good," Flynn said. "Then maybe you can help me. I've got some questions, too."

Chapter Thirty-Five

The next morning Clint had breakfast at Palmetto. He felt he should tell Arlo what was going on.

"Maggie's probably right," Arlo said. "Gator won't shoot her. You'll have a better chance of him talking to you with her along."

"I just didn't want you to feel I was leaving you out," Clint said.

"Hey, I've got work to do here, and I really don't want to go see Gator. He's more than a little crazy. Take that as a warning."

"I will," Clint said. "I figured anybody who wrestled alligators must be a little crazy."

"Anybody who lives in the swamp is a little crazy, too. But you oughtta see him wrestle one of them critters," Arlo said. "It's something to see, and he looks so happy while he's doing it."

"Maybe I'll get the chance."

He left Palmetto, fetched his horse from the livery where he'd boarded it, and rode to Maggie's house. There was already a horse tied outside. He tied his right next to it and went to the door.

When he knocked, she opened the door and stepped out. She was wearing boots, pants and what looked like a man's shirt.

"I'm dressed for the swamp," she said.

"But we're riding there, right?"

"Part way," she said. "We're also going to have to walk a ways."

"Through the swamp?"

"Oh yeah," she said. "But don't worry, you're dressed all right. It's important to be wearing boots."

They mounted up, and he gave her just a half a length's head start so he could follow.

***

They left the town limits, rode across some flatlands for a while, but finally came to a swampy area.

"This all empties out into the St. Johns River. But we just have to walk to Turnbull's Creek, not to the river."

They reined in and dismounted, tied their horses to a tree.

"Okay," she said. "It's about a half a mile walk. Just watch out for snakes and gators."

"Really? What kind of snakes?"

"Cottonmouths, diamondbacks mostly," she said. "Those are particularly venomous."

"And what kind of alligators?"

"It doesn't matter," she said. "A gator's a gator. They'll all bite you in half. It's a good thing you have your gun. Usually, I'd carry a rifle, but I'm with the Gunsmith."

They started walking through the swamp.

"What's Gator like?" he asked. "I mean, other than the fact that he wrestles alligators."

"Well, for one thing, he's huge."

"Tall, you mean?"

"No," she said, "huge, like a mountain. Yeah, he's tall, but he also weighs about three hundred pounds. Could you shoot that?"

"What?"

"That cottonmouth right there."

He looked up ahead, saw the cottonmouth hanging down from a tree, drew and fired, shooting it's head off.

"Now that's the Gunsmith I've read about," she said, impressed.

He ejected the spent shell, replaced it with a live one and holstered the gun.

"Didn't we just warn Gator that we're coming?" he asked.

"There's always shots being fired in the swamp," she told him. "Gator doesn't care."

They walked further without running into another snake or an alligator. There was water all around them, but Maggie seemed to be able to find some solid purchase.

Finally, they came within sight of a cabin. It seemed large enough to have just one room. Alongside the cabin were some racks with alligators of varying sizes hanging from them.

"Gator doesn't waste any part of the gators," she said. "After he gets all the meat, he makes use of the skins. But he has to hang them out to dry first.

As they got closer, Clint thought he saw alligators from three to six feet hanging.

Behind the shack was what looked like an outhouse, and also a shed.

"Do we knock?" he asked, as they reached the cabin.

"No," she said, "we just yell . . . Gaaatoooor!"

They stopped to listen, then Maggie called out again.

"Who's that?" a gruff voice called back.

"It's Maggie, Gator."

The door of the outhouse opened and a mountain of a man stepped out, pulling up his suspenders.

"Can't a man take a shit in peace?" he demanded.

"Now, Gator," Maggie said, "be polite. You have a new visitor."

Gator glared at Clint and the look literally made Clint's anus shrivel. After all, the man wrestled alligators.

Chapter Thirty-Six

"Who is he?" Gator asked.

"Clint Adams."

"Don't know 'im."

"I know that," Maggie said. "That's why I'm here, to introduce you."

"Well," the big man said, "go ahead, then."

"Gator," she said, "this is Clint Adams. Clint, this is Gator."

"Whataya want?" Gator demanded.

He had a mass of unruly black hair on his head, and black stubble covered the lower part of his face. Oddly, he had no eyebrows.

"I want to talk about Pelican Pete Davis."

"Maggie's husband," Gator said. "A fisherman, and a loser."

"Why's he a loser?"

Gator grinned, showing almost as many gaps as teeth.

"He lost Maggie, didn't he?" He cackled at that.

"Gator," Maggie said, "can we go inside?"

"You don't wanna do that, Mags," he said. "It stinks in there. Lemme go in, get a jug, and I'll be right back out."

"Okay," she said. "Do that."

Gator nodded and hurried into the shack. He came running back in moments carrying a jug.

"I make this myself," he said, "in a still I have further in the swamp. Come on, I got some benches over here."

They followed Gator to the other side of the shed, where there was a bench against the wall, and another across from it. He sat on the one against the shack wall, and his bulk seemed to shift the structure.

Clint and Maggie sat across from him.

"Swig?" he asked, holding the jug out.

Maggie accepted it and had a drink, then passed it to Clint. He sipped and handed it back to the big man, who took a healthy swallow.

"I'm gonna talk to ya," he said, then, "only because Maggie brung ya here."

"That's good enough for me," Clint said.

"So whataya want?"

"I've heard folks around here saying you might've killed Pelican Pete."

"First of all," Gator said, "why would I do that, and second, don't you think somebody my size woulda been seen down at the docks?"

He had a point. He would have been physically unable to sneak down there, kill Pete, and get away.

"Besides, I hate boats," Gator said.

"You use a boat in the swamp," Maggie said.

"Those are canoes," Gator said. "Or a flatboat. There's a difference."

Clint couldn't imagine the man's bulk in a canoe.

"Pete was killed with a blade," Clint said. "Do you know anyone else around here who uses blades, other than you?"

"Lots of men use knives," Gator said.

"What about your machete?" Clint asked. "Anybody else use a machete?"

"Probably not." The big man took another drink, then looked at Maggie. "Mags, I didn't kill 'im."

She looked at Clint.

"He didn't kill him."

"So you believe him?"

"Yes."

Clint looked at Gator.

"Damn it," he said, "so do I."

"Hey!" Gator said, surprisingly quick as he sprang to his feet, "you wanna go alligator huntin'?"

Clint didn't know if he was speaking to him, or to Maggie, but they both said, "No!"

"So that's it, then?" Gator asked. "Cause I gotta get back to work. There's an eight-footer out there waitin' for me."

"Eight feet?" Clint asked.

"Yeah," Gator said, "he's a beauty. You sure you don't wanna come?"

"Can I shoot it?" Clint asked.

"What? No, I'm gonna wrestle it!"

That might have been worth seeing, but Clint didn't think he could give that time away at the moment.

"Maybe after I find out who killed Pelican Pete."

"Why are you so interested?" Gator asked.

"He had something he was going to give me," Clint said.

"What was it?"

"I don't know. I searched the boat, but didn't find anything."

"Have you looked in his house?"

"His house?" Clint asked. "He had a house? I don't know why I thought he lived on his boat."

"He might as well have," Maggie said, "but I can take you to his house, if you want."

"Jesus," Clint said, "I should've thought of that in the first place."

Chapter Thirty-Seven

They walked back through the swamp to their horses and mounted up.

"So what did you think?" she asked, as they rode back to her house.

"He was . . . big," Clint said, "like you said, and I probably would've enjoyed seeing him wrestle that eight-footer, but that'll have to wait for another time."

"I don't think there'll be another time," Maggie said.

"No," he said, "I didn't really think so, either."

When they dismounted in front of her house she asked, "Do you want to come in?"

"Actually," he said, "I thought we'd go over to Pete's house so I could look around."

"Can we get some lunch first?" she asked.

"Sure. Palmetto's okay?"

"I was thinking of taking you someplace else," she said. "It's between here and Pete's, and we can walk."

"Oh, okay," he said. "I'm in your hands, so lead the way."

"Good," she said. "I think you'll like it."

***

He did like it, and it was his idea of normal food, not alligator or shrimp. He actually had one of the best plates of meat loaf he had ever had.

"Wow," he said, as he and Maggie left the place, "that was good."

"I thought maybe you'd like something you were more used to," she said. "Mama Nichols makes the best meat loaf."

"I believe it," Clint said.

"We can walk to Pete's house from here."

"Do you have a key?" he asked.

"No," she said, "will you need a key to get in?"

"Probably not."

"Then let's walk."

It was only fifteen minutes from Mama Nichols restaurant to Pelican Pete's little, rundown shack of a house. It was almost as small as Gator's.

They stopped at the front door.

"Is this the only way in?" he asked.

"It's the only door," she said. "We could use a window."

"No," Clint said, "the door's fine."

He pressed his shoulder to it, and it gave easily. When they walked in, he saw that the place was a mess.

"The door was locked," he said, but it looks like somebody was already here, searching."

"No," she said, "this is just the way he lived."

"Really?" Clint asked. "The boat was pretty neat."

"That's because the boat was his life," Maggie said, looking around with her arms folded. "This was just where he slept . . . sometimes."

"Well," Clint said, "I was hoping this was where he would keep something important."

"I don't know what Pete would do with something important," she said. "I never knew him to smuggle anything you'd call important. You don't have any idea what it was? Or how big it was?"

"No," Clint said, moving around the interior. It was one room, with a bed, a table and a couple of chairs, a chest of drawers and a pot-bellied stove that looked like it hadn't been used in some time.

He started looking under the mattress and the bed, inside the stove, inside the chest of drawers.

"Nothing?" she said.

"Nothing."

They sat at the table and looked at each other.

"What was Pete's usual contraband?" Clint asked.

"There are certain fish that are illegal," she said. "He'd smuggle those. Also, certain stones or metals . . . you know, but I don't really know what he was smuggling."

"And I don't know what he had for me," Clint said. "I'm thinking it might be time to leave Florida and head home. Nothing's turning out the way it was supposed to."

"What else were you supposed to do?" she asked.

He studied her for a moment, then figured, why not?

He told her about Geronimo asking to see him, and what the Apache medicine man wanted him to do.

"Wait," she said, "he has three wives in Fort Marion?"

"Apparently."

"That poor man," she said, "and I never thought I'd say that about someone who I only heard bad things about. So he's not a savage?"

"No," Clint said, "he's an honorable man."

"Wow," she said, shaking her head.

"Let's get out of here," he said, standing up.

They left the house together and pulled the door closed behind them.

"Did Pete have any family?" Clint asked, as they walked back to her house.

"No," she said, "I guess I'm the closest thing he had."

"So the house, the boat, they'll be yours?"

"I guess," she said. "But I don't want them, I know that."

When they reached her house, she turned to him and said, "So, you don't think you can do anything for Geronimo and his family?"

"Not personally," he said. "Maybe I can convince somebody in Washington to help, but I'd have to have something to trade."

"Like whatever it was you were supposed to get from Pete?" she asked.

"Maybe."

"You won't be leaving tonight, right?"

"No, not tonight."

"Do you want to come in?"

"I do, but I've got to take care of my horse and stop at my hotel."

"Well, just come back when you're finished," she said. "I'll cook something."

"Not alligator, okay?" he asked.

She smiled and said. "Okay, deal."

He grabbed his horse's reins.

"You want me to take your horse?" he asked.

"No, that's okay," she said. "I'll take care of him myself."

"I'll see you later, then," he said, and walked away, leading his horse.

Chapter Thirty-Eight

By the time he got back to his hotel, he had stopped thinking about Pelican Pete Davis and was back around to the Geronimo problem. When he entered the lobby, he was surprised to see Lieutenant Flynn sitting there.

"Mr. Adams," the young policeman said, standing. "I've been waiting for you."

"Why's that, Lieutenant?"

"We think we know who killed Pelican Pete," Flynn said.

"Is that right? Who?"

"A fella named Gator O'Neil," Flynn said. "He's supposed to wrestle alligators, but he also uses a machete."

"And was Pete killed with a machete?"

"Well, no, but he was stabbed."

"He didn't do it," Clint said.

"How do you know?"

"Because I talked to him today, and he said he didn't do it."

"And you believe him?"

"Yes."

"Well, my chief wants me to pick him up, so . . . you know where he lives?"

"Yes," Clint said, "in a swamp near Turnbull Creek."

"Can you take me there?"

"Actually, no."

"Why not? You were just there."

"Somebody took me," Clint said, "and I don't think I could find my way back."

"Why not?"

"Because it was the swamp, and it all looks the same to me," Clint said. "I mean, I've seen swamps before, but nothing like these Florida swamps."

"I didn't see swamps in Pennsylvania, either," Flynn admitted.

"Well," Clint said, "if you're going out there, wear high, thick boots, because you've got to watch out for the snakes and alligators."

"Snakes," Flynn said.

"And if you're going out there, you better take some men with you."

"Why's that?"

"Gator's six-and-a-half feet tall and three hundred pounds," Clint said.

"I was told he was big, but . . ."

"So big that if he was on the dock stabbing Pete, he would've been seen, don't you think?"

"Probably."

"So who told you he did it?"

"No one," Flynn said, "it was just my investigation—"

"If I was you," Clint said, "I'd investigate some more."

"Yeah," Flynn said, "okay . . ."

"Good luck."

He started for his room, leaving a confused looking Flynn standing there, but the desk clerk called him over.

"I've got a message for you."

"Who brought it in?"

"I dunno."

"When did it come?"

"I dunno," the clerk said. "It was here when I came in an hour ago."

"Okay," Clint said, accepting the sealed envelope, "thanks."

He waited til he got back to his room. It wasn't a telegram, just a hand-written note that said, IF YOU WANT WHAT PELICAN PETE HAD FOR YOU, MEET ME ON HIS BOAT AT MIDNIGHT. It wasn't signed.

"Shit," he said. It sounded like a trap, to him, but he couldn't afford to ignore it. Maybe it was on the level.

Chapter Thirty-Nine

He had no choice but to go alone.

Arlo was the owner of a restaurant, not someone he could count on to watch his back. Neither could he depend on Maggie to back his play. He could have gone to the sheriff, or to Lieutenant Flynn, but he didn't trust them. No, if this was a trap, he was going to have to walk into it and hope he could walk out again. But if it wasn't a trap, then maybe he'd be able to put his hands on whatever it was the government wanted from Pelican Pete. And once he had it, maybe he could turn things to his own advantage.

He stopped at the pier and looked around. Once again, moonlight was all he had to see by, but for the moment he didn't detect anyone else in the area. He touched his gun and started toward Pelican Pete's boat on one side, and a second boat on the other.

When he reached them, he looked behind him, then at the two boats. He didn't see anyone on Pelican Pete's. However, someone did appear on the second boat.

"Here."

"I thought we were meeting on Pete's boat?" Clint said.

"I felt safer over here," the man said.

"Is that your boat?"

"No, it belongs to someone else," the man said. "But I'm not damaging it."

"You want me to come over there," Clint said, "or will you step off?"

"I'll get off," the man said, and did so, with a graceful leap. When he was on the pier Clint realized he was young, spry, not tall. He was also holding something down alongside his leg, but it wasn't a weapon.

"What's your name?" Clint asked.

"Jonas."

"How old are you, Jonas?"

"I'm seventeen. You're Clint Adams?"

"That's right."

"The Gunsmith?"

"Yes."

"And you were here to see Pete?"

"That's right."

"He didn't know who was gonna meet with him," Jonas said. "Just that the government was sending somebody."

"Well," Clint said, "that somebody was me, only I got here too late."

"Pete was afraid that might happen," Jonas said. "That's why he gave it to me."

"Gave what to you?"

"This." He handed Clint something that looked like a rolled-up scroll about two feet long. It was what he had been holding against his leg.

"What is it?" Clint asked.

"I don't know," Jonas said. "Pete knew it was something the government would want, so he contacted them."

"Where's it from?" Clint asked, hefting it.

"Cuba."

Clint looked down at the scroll.

"So what is it?" Jonas asked.

"I don't know either," Clint said, "but it doesn't really matter."

"It doesn't?"

"No," Clint said. "It's something Pete found, something he wanted to give or sell to the government, and somebody wanted to stop him."

"So they killed 'im."

"But they didn't find this because you had it." Clint held up the scroll, continued to explain. "But now, you don't have it, anymore, but if I was you, I'd still keep my head down."

"And what are you gonna be doin' in the meantime?" Jonas asked.

"Well, I'm going to get this to the right people," Clint said, "and I'm still going to try to find out who killed Pelican Pete."

"Who killed him?"

"Yeah."

"Well . . . I know who killed him."

Clint hesitated.

"You do?" he asked.

"Well, sure," Jonas said.

"How do you know?"

"I saw it happen."

"Where were you?"

"I was right there, on Pete's boat," Jonas explained, pointing. "He told me to hide when somebody came down the pier toward us."

"Was it a big guy? Like Gator O'Neil?"

"What? No, it wasn't Gator."

"Then who was it, Jonas?" Clint asked. "Who stabbed Pelican Pete?"

"It was a little guy," Jonas said. "Maybe you know 'im?"

"I don't know til you tell me his name."

"It was Arlo," Jonas said. "Arlo Crowder."

Chapter Forty

Clint walked up to Palmetto.

It was late, and the front door was locked, but he could see Arlo inside, cleaning up. He knocked on the door and the little man came over.

"Hey," Arlo said, "come on in. You're lucky I'm here this late. I had to do some cleaning."

Clint entered and Arlo locked the door again.

"What's been happening?" Arlo asked.

"Not much," Clint said. "I found what Pelican Pete was going to give me."

"You did?"

"Yup."

"What was it?"

"This." Clint held the scroll up.

"What is it?"

"I don't know," Clint said. "I'm going to let somebody else worry about that."

"Why not open it?"

Clint shook his head.

"Not interested."

"What are you interested in, then?" Arlo asked.

"Nothing," Clint said. "I've got all the answers."

"Do you?" Arlo asked, grabbing his broom. "Keep talkin', I've got to take this into the kitchen. Tell me what else you know."

"I know who killed Pete," Clint said.

"Oh yeah?" Arlo called from the kitchen. "Who?"

"You, Arlo."

It was quiet in the kitchen, and just when Clint thought Arlo may have gone out a back way, he came through the door holding a gun in his hand.

"You're not going to deny it?" Clint asked.

"What's the point?" Arlo asked. "How'd you find out?"

"You were seen."

"By who?"

"That's not important."

"Jonas," Arlo said. "It had to be."

"Has that thing been fired lately?" Clint asked, indicating the Colt in Arlo's hand.

"Recently enough for me to know it works," Arlo said.

"Why'd you use a knife on Pete?"

"I wanted to get close enough," Arlo said, "and I wanted people to think it was Gator."

"Well, you can forget that now."

"Why's that?"

"Because I know, and Jonas knows."

"But I'm taking care of you now, and Jonas later," Arlo said.

"Is that right?" Clint asked. "Tell me something, Arlo. Why'd you kill Pete?"

"Two reasons," Arlo said. "One, I knew he had found something valuable."

"How'd you know that?"

"He told me," Arlo said. "He came in here one day, ate, and told me."

"And the second reason?"

"I didn't like him anymore."

"Why?"

"He told me my alligator was dry."

"What?"

"That alligator I made for you?" Arlo said. "He said it was dry."

"You killed him because he criticized your cooking?"

"Well," Arlo said. "mainly it was for what he found that was valuable. See, I'm tired of cooking for these people. I'm tired of alligator, and turtle soup, conch, shrimp . . . I want to get out of St. Augustine, but for that I need money." He pointed with the barrel of his gun at the scroll Clint was holding. "That's going to get me out."

"I don't think so," Clint said.

"Why not?" Arlo asked. "You don't think it's worth anything?"

"I don't really know," Clint said. "I just know that you're not getting your hands on it."

"Really?" Arlo asked. "I know you're an old West legend and all, but I happen to be holding a gun on you."

"But you have no experience with guns, do you?" Clint asked. "Knives are probably more your thing."

"Yeah, they are," Arlo said, "but that doesn't mean I can't pull a trigger."

"All I'm saying is that you can't pull the trigger fast enough," Clint said.

"I already have my gun in my hand," Arlo said. "I know how fast the dime novels say you are, but nobody's that fast."

"Arlo," Clint said, "you've got two choices."

"Yeah? What are they?"

"Come with me to the sheriff's office," Clint said, "or pull that trigger now."

"I'm not turning myself in," Arlo said, "so . . ."

Clint saw Arlo's eyes narrowing and knew he was about to pull the trigger, so he drew and fired once. The bullet struck Arlo in the chest, staggering him and then freezing him in place. Slowly, his hand opened, and the gun fell to the floor.

"Damn," he said, his eyes wide, "that was fast . . ."

Chapter Forty-One

Clint sat in a chair across the desk from Sheriff Roy Jensen.

"I would've contacted you, but it was late, and I didn't know where you lived, so I had to go to the police. They took care of the body. They wanted me to come back today and talk with Lieutenant Flynn."

"Then why are you here now?" Jensen asked.

"Because I don't think Arlo was in this alone."

"Why not?"

"I just didn't accept his reasons for what he did," Clint said.

"So you think someone else put him up to it?"

"Yes."

"Who?"

"That's what I was hoping you could help me figure out."

"Why me?" the sheriff asked.

"Because the only other person I knew in St. Augustine who might help me out was Arlo."

"Ah," Jensen said. "And what about the . . . what are we calling it?"

"The package."

"What about this package you're not telling me much about?" the sheriff asked.

"It's in a safe place," Clint said. "I sent a telegram this morning."

"So somebody's coming to pick it up?"

"Yes."

"But you think there's a person out there who still might want to take it away from you."

"That's what I think."

"And why do you think I'd have some ideas who that might be?"

"I don't," Clint said. "I think whoever it is will show themselves to me soon enough, and I'll handle it. But you and Arlo have lived here a long time. Who was he close to?"

"Yeah," Jensen said, "Arlo and me, we go back a ways."

"I thought you might."

Jensen stared at Clint, then smiled.

"I get it now," he said.

"What's that?"

"You think it's me," Jensen said. "You think I sent Arlo to kill Pete."

"Like I said," Clint replied. "You and Arlo have been here a long time."

"What did you tell the police?"

"Just that I had to kill Arlo, and that he killed Pete."

"Nothing about me?"

"I woke this morning and this popped into my head," Clint said. "I wasn't thinking about you last night."

Jensen sat back and looked around.

"Most days," he said, "this feels like a coffin."

"I can see why."

"Yeah," Jensen said, "I've been looking for a way out for a long time."

"And Pelican Pete was it?"

"Pete was the only friend I had in town," Jensen said. "That was why I couldn't kill him myself."

"Why have him killed at all?" Clint asked.

"When he came in that day and said he'd found something valuable, he couldn't keep his mouth shut about it," Jensen said. "He said he was going to sell it to the government."

"So you enlisted Arlo."

"He was a good cook," Jensen said, "And a very good man with a blade."

"Well, he wasn't very good with a gun," Clint said. "How about you?"

"This is not the Wild West, Mr. Adams," Jensen said. "I'm not about to try and draw down on you."

"Good choice."

"But I'm also not going anywhere with you," Jensen said.

"I didn't think you were."

"So where do we stand?" Jensen asked.

"I'm going to tell Lieutenant Flynn about you," Clint said.

"What can you prove?"

"Nothing," Clint said. "I'm going to tell him what I think. The rest is up to him."

"What do you think he'll do with it?"

"That's not my business," Clint said. "I'll be long gone."

"How do I know you won't shoot me in the back before you leave?" Jensen asked.

"I don't care what you've read or heard about me," Clint said, "you never heard that I ever shot anyone in the back."

"No," Jensen said, "you're right about that."

"I also don't take kindly to anyone trying to bushwhack me," Clint added.

"Yeah, I heard that," Jensen said.

Clint stood up.

"I only came here to give you a chance," he said.

"A chance to do what?"

"Turn yourself in."

"To Flynn?" Jensen asked. "Do you know he was a teacher before he got this job? A teacher! And you want me to turn myself in to him?"

"Like I said," Clint replied, "it's your choice."

Jensen fell silent and Clint left the coffin-like office.

Chapter Forty-Two

Clint went directly to the police department building.

"Mr. Adams!" the young policeman on the front desk greeted him. "I'm sorry, sir. The last time you were here I didn't know who you were."

"That's okay," Clint said. "Is Flynn around? I'm supposed to meet with him today."

"Oh, sure. I'll take you back there."

Clint followed the kid to Flynn's office, found the man sitting behind his desk, his eyes closed.

"Thanks, kid," he said to the officer.

He entered the office and Flynn opened his eyes.

"Adams."

"Lieutenant," Clint said. "Sorry to wake you."

"I'm not used to being woke up in the middle of the night," Flynn said. "I guess I'll have to get used to that in this job."

"Didn't happen when you were a teacher, did it?" Clint asked.

"No, it didn't," he said. "What can I do for you?"

"Well, we didn't get a chance to talk last night," Clint said. "I mean, I talked to your young officer out there, and he woke you up, and you had some men move the body, but you wanted me to come in today and tell you what happened, exactly," he reminded the Lieutenant.

"Right, right." Flynn wiped his face with both hands. "Okay, tell me the whole story, from the beginning."

Clint started at the beginning, took Flynn all the way through to his meeting that morning with Sheriff Jensen.

"So you're here on behalf of the government."

"Right."

"Can you show me this thing, this package that Pelican Pete had for you?"

"No, I can't," Clint said. "I have to turn it over to the government. If they want to show it to you, that's up to them."

"So, is someone coming down here, or are you taking it to Washington?"

"You don't have to worry about that," Clint said. "What are you going to do about Jensen?"

"What can I do?" Flynn said. "Do you have any proof?"

"Just what he told me."

"And the two of you were alone when he told you," Flynn said. "Look, I know I'm new to this job, but my chief's not going to let me do anything without proof."

"Well, I'm just telling you what I know, Lieutenant," Clint said, standing. "The rest is up to you."

"Let me tell you what *I* know," Flynn said. "You killed a man last night."

"I told you why and how that happened."

"I'm telling you not to leave town," Flynn said. "Not yet, anyway."

"Lucky for you," Clint said, "I wasn't intending to."

Clint turned and left the office.

***

He walked past Palmetto, which had been locked up since Arlo's death. Then he went to Maggie's house. She let him in, then collected the package from where she had hidden it for him.

"Thanks," he said.

'Don't you want to know if I looked at it?"

"No," he said. "I know you didn't."

"How did you know you could trust me?" she asked.

"Arlo and the sheriff turned out to be involved," he answered. "I figured my odds were pretty good that you weren't."

She handed him the scroll.

"What will you do now?"

"That's easy," he said. "Wait."

***

When he got to his hotel, he stopped at the front desk to talk to the clerk.

"Has anybody been looking for me?" he asked.

"No, sir."

"Well, if somebody is, let them come up."

"Yes, sir."

He had only sent a telegram to Washington that morning, so there was probably no chance anybody would come for "the package" that day. But there was always a chance somebody else might come.

He went to his room and made sure the door was locked, then sat on the bed and took the package and put it on the pillow. Then he put his gun down next to it and started reading FRANKENSTEIN.

***

He heard the floor outside his room creaking before he heard anything else. A glance at the window told him it was getting on toward dusk. He put the book down, placed the scroll under the pillow, and picked up his gun. When the knock came at the door, he carried the gun to it, stood off to one side in case a bullet or a machete came through.

"Who is it?"

Chapter Forty-Three

He opened the door and let Jeremy Pike in.

"You made good time," Clint said.

"I was actually in Atlanta on another matter," Pike said. "When I got the telegram from Washington, I headed right down here."

Clint closed the door, walked to the bed and put the gun back on the pillow.

"So," Pike said, "do you have the, uh, item?"

"I do," Clint said.

"Can I see it?"

"Not yet."

"Why not?"

"We have to come to an understanding, first," Clint told him.

"An understanding?"

"Yes."

"About what?" Pike asked.

"About me being lied to," Clint said.

"Ah, Clint—"

"Lied to by General Hammond, and then by you," Clint said. "I only hope Jim wasn't in on this."

"He wasn't."

"Good."

"We just wanted to get you down here—"

"So you lied about Geronimo."

"No," Pike said, "no, that wasn't a lie, uh, exactly. He did ask to see you—"

"—the government just had no intentions of honoring his requests."

"That's uh, pretty much it," Pike said. "I'm sorry, Clint, but I had orders—"

"Never mind," Clint said, "being lied to isn't so foreign to me, but now *I* have demands."

"Demands?"

"Which will have to be met before I turn the package over to you."

"I, uh, don't know that I can agree to demands—"

"—then you'll have to send a telegram, won't you?"

Pike sat down on the edge of the bed.

"Okay, what are your demands?"

"Before we even get to that," Clint said, "tell me what this scroll is."

"Scroll?"

"Pike—"

"Okay, all right," Pike said. "I suppose you deserve to know, but don't tell anybody I told you."

"I've got nobody to tell."

"During the civil war the fort was attacked by Confederate ships. The cannons pretty much took care of the problem, but the Confederate boats had something of value on them."

"Like what?"

"Like gold."

"And it's still at the bottom?"

"It's somewhere," Pike said. "Apparently, the tide moved it all, and that scroll is a map showing where it is."

"And you believe that?"

"Doesn't matter if I believe it or not," Pike said. "Pelican Pete contacted Washington, said he found it, and Washington wanted it." He spread his hands. "That's it."

"Jesus," Clint said, "that's a bunch of crap."

"Can we discuss your demands, now?"

***

When Clint returned to Pensacola he stayed in the same hotel.

"Welcome back, sir," the clerk said.

"Thank you. How did things go with the boys?"

"Oh, they remained with us til the end of the week," the clerk explained. "When the doctor left, he gave them the okay to move."

"Have you seen them since?"

"No."

Clint realized he never knew where the McBain boys lived. They simply met him in front of the train station, and the hotel.

"Okay, thanks."

Clint went to his room. At least he knew the boys were all right when they left the hotel. He could check in with Constable Snyder to see if he knew where the boys were, but he had something else to do first.

***

When he got off the ferry on Santa Rosa Island the pilot commented. "Don't usually see folks comin' back here a second time."

"You won't see me here a third time, that's for sure," Clint assured him.

He walked up to Fort Pickens and was shown to the warden's office. Warden Horace Watson greeted him with a handshake, and then they sat.

"So, what brings you back here, Mr. Adams?" the warden asked.

"How much did you know about my previous visit?" Clint asked.

"What do you mean?"

"Did you know that the government had no intention of honoring any of Geronimo's requests?"

"I only knew you were coming because Geronimo requested it. I didn't know the details."

Clint wondered if the same was true of Lieutenant Colonel Langdon, at Fort Marion?

"I need to see Geronimo again."

"I've been instructed to permit it," the warden said, rising from his chair. "If you'll just wait here, I'll have him brought to you."

"I'd also like the same conditions as last time," Clint said.

"Of course," Watson said. "I'll have the food brought in as well."

Clint nodded, and as Warden Watson left the office, he settled back in his chair to wait for the Apache medicine man to arrive.

Chapter Forty-Four

The food and drink came first, and then Geronimo was ushered in, again in chains.

"The chains," Clint said.

As before, only the wrists were freed. His feet remained chained.

"Thank you," Clint said.

The warden turned and walked his men out.

Geronimo sat, grabbed a piece of meat.

"I was not sure you would return," he said.

"I thought you asked for me because I was the only white man you could trust."

"I can't trust any whites," Geronimo corrected, "but you are the closest I have come."

"I suppose I should be flattered."

"You have returned from Fort Marion," Geronimo said.

"Yes."

"Did you see my family there?"

"I didn't see them, but I spoke with the Warden about them."

The old Apache snagged another piece of meat and chewed.

"And what did he say?"

"Nothing good."

Geronimo stood.

"I will go back to my cell."

"No," Clint said, "sit, please."

Geronimo sat and stared.

"I made a deal with the government," Clint said. "I didn't have to deal with the warden who, quite frankly, is an Indian hater."

"As are most whites."

"Well, I made a discovery down there that allowed me to broker a deal. As a result, your wives and children are being taken from Fort Marion—"

"And brought here?" Geronimo showed emotion for the first time.

"No," Clint said, "they're being taken to the Mount Vernon Barracks in Alabama. There is more space there, better conditions, and it's closer to here. So, at some point, you may be able to see them."

"And this was promised to you?"

"It was."

"There have been many promises broken by the whites to my people."

"Not this one," Clint said. "In fact, I'm sure that, as we speak, your wives and children are already there."

"But you have not seen this yourself."

"No," Clint answered, uncomfortably.

Geronimo stared at him.

"You have taken the word of others," he said, finally, "and I must take your word for this."

"Yes."

"And you are satisfied?"

Clint thought a moment, then said, "No, actually, I'm not."

"Ah . . ."

"Geronimo," Clint said, "I will go to Mount Vernon and see for myself. I will then send you a message."

"How will I know the message is from you?"

"It will be worded a special way," Clint said. "When you hear those words, you will know it is from me."

"And what will those words be?"

"We will agree on that before I leave here today," Clint said. "But before that, you must tell me how I will recognize your family."

"You believe they might show you any Indian women with their children and tell you they are mine."

"It's possible."

"Then listen closely . . ."

***

Clint left Fort Pickens and went back to Pensacola. He had not yet returned the rented horse to Jamie, but now he needed it to ride to Alabama. Before that, however, he realized he could find out about the McBain boys from the hostler, and not from the constable.

He stopped by the large barn and walked through the open front doors. Jamie, while shoeing a horse, looked up, saw him and straightened.

"You're back." He looked behind Clint. "And so's my horse."

"Didn't you think we would be?"

Jamie shrugged and said, "I wasn't sure."

"We need to renegotiate," Clint said. "I'll be needing the horse a bit longer. I have to go to Alabama."

"No problem," Jamie said. "Same deal."

"That suits me. By the way, have you seen Kenny and Danny since I left?"

"Yeah, I have."

"Are they doing okay?"

"They're fine," Jamie said. "Danny's healing, and they're staying out of trouble."

"That's good."

"Do you want to see them before you leave again?"

"No," Clint said, "that's okay. Oh, what can you tell me about Eddie Garvin?"

"Oh," Jamie said, "he's out of business, and moved on."

"That's good to hear."

"Sure you don't wanna see the boys?" Jamie asked. "I can tell 'em I seen ya."

"Go ahead and tell them, but make sure they understand I couldn't stay. Tell them it had to do with Geronimo."

"I'll tell 'em."

"Listen," Clint said. "Let's come to terms on a sale price for your horse and saddle. I won't be coming back from Alabama, and I'll probably sell them before I head back west."

"Sure," Jamie said, "come on back to the office and let's do it."

***

The next morning, Clint mounted the mare and left Pensacola, bound for Alabama, after seeing Geronimo's wives and children at the Mount Vernon Barracks, he sent a telegram to Washington D.C.

A few days later, the warden had Geronimo brought into his office. There was no food and drink, this time.

"You have a telegram, but nobody here knows what it means," he said.

"What does it say?" the Apache medicine man asked.

"Something about eagles in the nest," Watson said. "Do you know what that means?"

"I do."

Watson looked at the two guards and said, "Take the Chief back to his cell."

Coming April 27, 2020

THE GUNSMITH
458
The Gunsmith Saloon

For more information
visit: www.SpeakingVolumes.us

On Sale Now!

THE GUNSMITH
456
The Daughter of Jean Lafitte

**For more information
visit:** www.SpeakingVolumes.us

On Sale Now!

THE GUNSMITH *series*
Books 430 - 455

**For more information
visit:** www.SpeakingVolumes.us

Coming Soon!

Lady Gunsmith
9
Roxy Doyle and the Lady Executioner

For more information
visit: www.SpeakingVolumes.us

On Sale Now!

Lady Gunsmith
Books 1 - 8
Roxy Doyle and the Silver Queen

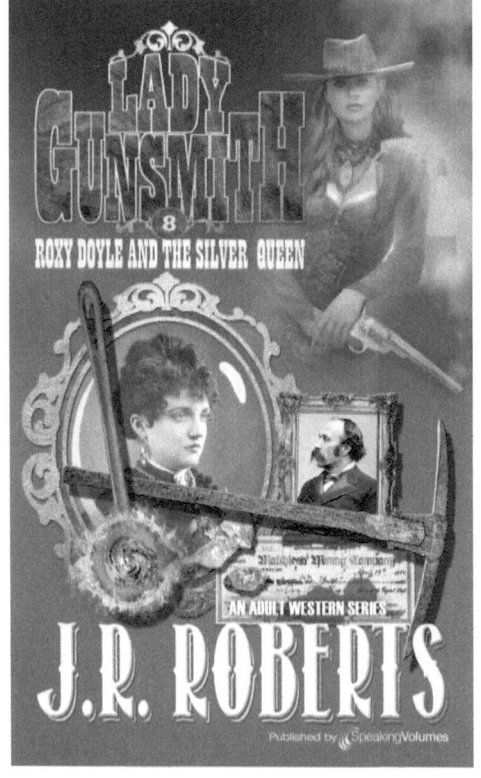